SECONDARY ROADS

STRANGE STORIES

———— ♦ ————

C.M. Muller

CHTHONIC MATTER | St. Paul, Minnesota

SECONDARY ROADS
Strange Stories

© 2022 by C.M. Muller

FIRST EDITION

Cover art by Yaroslav Gerzhedovich (Shutterstock)

Additional proofreading by Chris Mashak

Fonts: Spectral, Roadway

CHTHONIC MATTER | St. Paul, Minnesota
www.chthonicmatter.wordpress.com

CONTENTS

A WINTER REUNION

———◆———

HUNCHED FORWARD, hands tense on the wheel, Ing searched the swirling white expanse for signs of movement, a taillight, anything to indicate that he was not experiencing this godforsaken snowstorm alone. He was traveling under thirty miles an hour, and even this was beginning to feel uncomfortable. His back ached and the radio no longer functioned as it should, emitting various shades of static. The snow had begun falling not long after he had crossed the state line, and it had only worsened as the miles ticked by. While he had taken the trip to Hettinger on numerous occasions, never had he done so during winter.

There was little doubt that Leva and the rest of them were already worrying over his whereabouts. In a perfect world, in a world without all this misery-inducing snow, Ing would have arrived in town by now, reminiscing about old times and nursing his first aquavit. But the botched weather report couldn't be blamed on forecasters alone. No, the one who deserved an earful was his sister, who had decided to organize this year's Enger family reunion in the middle of January. And yes, as she had explained to him over the phone, there was an important historical reason for doing so.

From an early age, Leva had been fascinated with the past. She could sit for hours in their grandfather's lap, listening to the old man spin his folkloric and familial tales. Ing knew exactly what the elder would have called the event currently transpiring beyond the Volvo's frost-covered windows: *Fimbulvetr*, that apocalyptic winter said to be prelude to the end of the world. Ing had enjoyed the tales nearly as much as his sister, even if in retrospect they seemed antiquated, belonging to a time when the mysteries of the world were centuries from being solved. Nevertheless, he was grateful for the memories he shared with Leva. There was a comfort there, tranquility that in his old age he had never been able to replicate. At certain times he had longed to retreat to that cozy Enger living room with its fireplace and wingback chairs, merely to listen to his grandfather recite some Asbjørnsen and Moe. Had the old man been along for the ride, it would not have seemed half so bad.

Then again, if Ing truly had his choice of traveling companions, his dear departed Ethel would have topped the list. Her death that past October had been a blow from which he knew he could never fully recover. Even if he managed to cull another decade from life, the joy that had been Ethel would continue to haunt him. Her passing had been unexpected because even at sixty-eight she had been the picture of health. She had more energy than most people half her age, and Ing had always assumed he would be the first to go. Ideally, they would have gone together.

With Ethel, the trip would have been an ever-joyous and agreeable undertaking. She would have already started massaging his neck, relieving the tension there, venturing now and again to tickle an ear. Ing missed her gentle touch and her soft, intelligent voice. She could talk for hours on end if the situation called for it, and never once repeat herself. Her easy-going nature and kind-heartedness would have lessened the monotony of the drive, and the snowstorm would have been made into a heavenly phenomenon.

Ing tried to remember when he had last seen a motorist's tail-light. It felt as though hours had passed. The intensity of the storm had boxed him into a padded cell of solitude, and while he felt sure that numerous other vehicles were not far ahead or behind, he sensed that he was traversing this stretch of nothingness alone. Snow had already drifted over much of the road, making it difficult to tell where it and the land came together. Not wishing to misjudge this boundary and end up in a culvert, Ing carefully eased the Volvo to the right as much as he dared and parked. Idling there, he peered nervously in the side and rearview mirrors, fearful of a rear-end collision.

A minute became five, but nothing emerged from *Fimbulvetr's* churning maw. Even though the Volvo's heater was going full blast, Ing was starting to lose sensation in his toes. He still had half a tank of gas, and he could sit at the edge of the road for a few more hours if necessary, but if the snow continued at its present rate there might come a point where rescue would be impossible. As if to will the luminous monstrosities into existence, Ing imagined a pair of snowplows racing in-sync across the frozen waste, patrol cars not far behind with officers on the lookout for stranded motorists.

Had he abided Leva's recommendation about obtaining a cell phone—"Nothing fancy, something for emergencies, something to tuck into the glove box"—Ing might have been able to call emergency services. A voice, even if it belonged to someone he did not know, would be of great comfort. But, as with everything involving new technology, he had stubbornly refused. As always, he was left with his wits, which at present were rapidly failing him.

As he tried the radio again, Ing grew disheartened by its ceaseless scan. Clicking it off, he focused instead on the eerily-similar static of the howling wind. It seemed to shift directions at will, determined to find a way inside the Volvo. Snow was blowing with such force it was beginning to feel as though a part of the world had dissolved. Ing wondered if he would experience a similar fate by stepping outside. The car was a safe haven, but it also represented little more than limbo. And *Fimbulvetr* would soon have its way.

Ing thought of the old Enger homestead where the reunion was to take place. While it was now fully incorporated into a "living history" exhibit, the rough-hewn shack had once stood alone in the middle of open prairie, on land claimed by his great-grandfather in 1864. Leva's rationale for holding the reunion in such an unforgiving month was simple. She wished to recall the year that had nearly wiped out the entire clan. It had been the first winter the family had experienced in their new home, and it had been a devastating one, particularly as it involved the loss of two children. Ing could well imagine the fear and helplessness that his forebears must have gone through. They had been as isolated as he was now, but they had had each other and persevered. He had no one, nothing but his memories.

Then again, if he managed to survive, he would have a spectacular tale to tell. One for the generations. Ing laughed at the absurdity, and it felt surprisingly good to do so. He closed his eyes and took a deep breath and readjusted the seat into a more comfortable position. He tried to clear his mind, tried to think of a way out of this wintery mess, but memories of Ethel kept coming to the fore. To have spent so many years with someone only to have that joy fall into a daily ritual of absence was nearly too much to bear. Ing felt tears welling in his eyes and to distract himself he turned toward the passenger seat, willing Ethel into existence. He needed her now if only to tell him that everything would be okay, that the storm would soon pass and the sun would shine again. As things stood, he would be buried alive in this Scandinavian steel coffin without a marker to remember him by.

His thoughts getting the better of him, Ing turned his attention to the side-view mirror. He needed to remain focused on the present, not memories, needed to keep an eye out for help. Someone would eventually chance on him, but until that time he needed to remain positive, as Ethel would have. He knew that she would want him to keep tethered to hope for as long as he was able. Never would she have allowed him to give in to despair.

It seemed to have grown darker. Ing checked his watch, thrilled to discover—even if every other aspect of his life had failed—it still worked. He held it to his ear, comforted by its steady click. Ethel had given it to him over fifty years ago, and the act of winding it each morning had always enlivened him, brought solace to his day. And while it was still hours from needing to be rewound, Ing did so anyway.

Suddenly, a figure scurried past the Volvo.

Ing refocused his attention, hoping for another glimpse, but the storm had already concealed the visitor. Ing uncoupled his seatbelt and, without thinking, lumbered outside. He pushed against the piercing wind to the front of the vehicle, calling as loudly as he could. The snow stung his forehead and eyes, and he was on the verge of turning back when he glimpsed a light in the far distance. It was part of an ill-defined structure about forty yards away, but as Ing squinted, hoping to see it more clearly, the shifting wind blotted it from view.

The point of light, however, remained, a star reflected in this arctic ocean. Ing was certain now more than ever that someone needed his help. A stranded motorist had made the foolish mistake, as he was making now, of leaving their vehicle in a desperate attempt to seek rescue. More than likely they were already suffering hypothermia. How else to explain that they had walked right past the Volvo.

Ing cursed the maelstrom, tightening his meager hood and proceeding toward the light. He glanced down, surprised by all the undisturbed snow. While it continued to accumulate at an unbelievable rate, there still should have been some sign of a disturbance. He moved ahead, continuing his sustained plea, encouraging the unseen motorist to approach his voice if they could hear. By the time he had ventured twenty paces, he half turned to ascertain the location of the Volvo, but it was already gone, absorbed into the void. Losing sight of that boxy but reliable refuge unnerved Ing. Nevertheless, he pushed on.

"Fimbulvetr . . . "

He stopped in his tracks, startled by the close-sounding voice. As he stared ahead, the structure he had previously glimpsed grew more defined. The front door was about ten yards away, and if no one was home or it turned out to be abandoned, Ing felt confident he could backtrack to his vehicle without much effort. The storm hadn't pushed him too far off course.

"Fimbulvetr . . . "

This time it was Ing who uttered the word, as though its recitation might bind him to the lost soul, might bring them together. He lumbered ahead, his pace infuriatingly slow. Snow continued to scrape his exposed flesh, making it difficult to focus for more than a second or two. He brought a hand up to shield his eyes and noticed a more expansive light emanating from a previously obscured window. Through its lit pane, the interior of the shack looked cozy and inviting, which was at odds with what he was expecting.

Ing strode to the front door, heartened by his good fortune. He knocked too heavily and the latch gave way, leaving the semi-open space collecting with snow. Without a thought, he stepped over the threshold and closed the door. The screaming storm was muted, and this new silence was unsettling. Lodged in *Fimbulvetr's* throat for so long had made its absent howl nearly as excruciating.

"Is anyone here?" Ing called, still lingering near the door. Judging by the silence, his abrupt entrance had startled the occupant into hiding.

It wasn't any warmer inside, but, without the wind, it felt less intense. Ing could still see his breath, and now that his eyes had adjusted he was shocked by the simplicity of the one-room shack. It wasn't half as appealing as it had appeared from the outside. There was a potbellied stove in the nearest corner, though its hearth was lifeless and no kindling was in sight. Next to this stood an immigrant chest, with a name scripted in gothic lettering across the front. It was irrevocably faded, and Ing doubted he could decipher it even up close. A table and two benches were set along the nearest wall, atop which rested a leatherbound book. Ing's grandfather had had a similar *bibelen* that he had treasured to his dying day. The only other visible furniture was a rocking chair and a spinning wheel.

Ing recalled the light that had originally drawn him inside, and only now did he think to search for its source. As far as he could tell there wasn't a lamp or candle burning anywhere, nothing that might have produced that painterly ambiance he had originally seen.

"Fimbulvetr . . . "

It was the same voice he had heard from outside, but this time it was accompanied by a tattered cough and soft moan. As he stepped toward the source, Ing noticed a dark blanket draped from the ceiling in a corner of the room, in effect creating a hidden space.

"I'm here to help," Ing said, his voice as gentle as he could manage. He pulled the blanket slowly to the side, not wanting to scare the individual any more than he already had. There was a bed beyond the curtain and laying on it, half curled into a fetal position, was an elderly woman. She was wearing nothing more than a ragged nightgown.

Ing knelt to have a closer look, wondering if the elder was even aware of his presence. He cleared his throat. "I saw you wandering outside and . . . " Even as he said this, he knew it could not be true. There was no way this frail creature could have trudged for any length of time through *Fimbulvetr*. No, she had not left this bed, this place, in a long time.

The old woman shifted toward Ing's voice, moaning as she repositioned herself to meet his eyes. Her own were startlingly familiar, reminding him of Ethel.

"It's going to be all right. My car's not too far away. I'll take you there." Ing stood up and undid the blanket from the ceiling. Once it was loose, he tucked an edge under the old woman and did his best to wrap all but her face. He lifted her into his arms, surprised not by his strength but by her lightness. She weighed hardly more than the blanket.

"I'm going to get you some help," he continued, struggling past the door and stepping into a miracle. The blizzard had stopped. *Fimbulvetr* had moved on.

Ing was heartened by the clarity and closeness of the Volvo. And the snow, unbelievably, did not seem as deep as he remembered. The sun was visible, but even its paltry rays could not have altered the landscape so rapidly. A semi blasted past his field of vision, scattering snow in its wake. It was gone before he thought to call out after it.

When he reached the Volvo, Ing was nearly overcome by the growing weight of his burden. Impossible as it seemed, the old woman felt heavier. Ing opened the passenger door and situated the elder in the seat. She peered at him and smiled, her face reborn in this new light.

"I'm appreciative of your kindness," she said, her voice clearer, more youthful-sounding. She looked so different now that she had been removed from her decrepit abode. This was no longer the withered old woman Ing had rescued.

"I don't think it's too far to the next town," he said. "We'll get help for you there." He shut the door and walked around to the other side, nearly losing his balance along the way. By the time he slipped inside and latched his seatbelt, he felt exhausted and uncertain about his ability to drive. Nevertheless, he put the car into gear and pulled slowly forward.

It was miles until he saw the first sign indicating a town and miles more before he felt a hand gently massaging his neck and moving up to tickle his ear. He turned toward the old woman, seeing in her further aspects of Ethel. Her cheeks, her smile . . .

"I'd been there so long," she said, her eyes glistening like a newborn's. "So long, in that dark, dark place, waiting for someone to come. And then you did." Her smile widened.

A final coherent thought came to Ing before he returned his attention, however wearily, to the road. He would have done well to have left the crone in her rotting bed. She hadn't been sick. He knew that now. Knew it with the same clarity that he knew he was on the decline, that in a short span *he* would be the one curled up and courting death. Darkness and further isolation were fast approaching, with the growing intensity of a winter storm.

But for now, Ing tried to enjoy the sensation at his neck, its tenderness reminding him of Ethel and death, entwined now as they were. He had a feeling that by the time those fingers ceased their magic and withdrew from his flesh, something else inside of him would end as well.

The creature at his side was humming, the intonation of which sounded mythic and warm, a song belonging to more ancient times, a melody evoking mysteries that only Ing's forebears could fully appreciate and comprehend.

If he listened long enough, he too might understand.

VANPOOL

———◆———

THE BOY AT THE WINDOW watches the rusty black van pull into the drive, its grimy tires stenciling snakeskin impressions over immaculate asphalt. The van crawls to a halt, mired, at least in the boy's imagination, in a pit of tar. Its internal belts squeal like a cry for help. While his first impulse is to crank shut the window, he instead hesitates, mesmerized by a rapidly expanding trail of exhaust. It appears sentient, an agent of the van whose sole function might be to analyze new environs, assess risk. Beneath this coiling tentacular mass, which seems now to have fixed on his location, the boy manages to glimpse his father striding toward the van, his black suit as flawless as the newly-laid drive. By the time he arrives at the opposite side of the vehicle, everything but his head disappears from view. Its features are spit-shined to perfection, like some corporate trophy. A hand crawls from the void, acknowledging the boy's presence with a slow-motion wave. Then, in a violent countermove, it tugs at his father's earlobe, forceful enough to remove his head from view. The boy can't be sure that the hand belonged to his father, and as the horror of this possibility sets in, he is jolted back to reality by the sound of a sliding door slamming shut. For a small eternity, the boy is left to wonder if the vehicle will ever depart or if it has anchored itself to the drive for an eight-hour shift, a mobile workplace. His father had been honest with him that things would be different from here on out, that the family would need to go through a period of adjustment. *Things will be different until they are familiar once again*, were his father's exact words. The boy turns now from the window to mark the time on the clock next to his bed, and as he returns to the dark tableau, the van has already reversed into the street. The windows are so dark as to offer no silhouettes, no inkling that his father resides within. As the van springs forward, its rear end bottoms out, bumper scraping the road like a knife pressed to sharpening-stone.

LATER THAT EVENING, as the boy reads in bed by nightlight, the van marks its return, far later than he or his mother expected. He tosses the book aside and struggles to free himself from the summer sheets. They cling with a will of their own, delaying his arrival at the window. The exhaust-agent has already infiltrated his room through the screen, sending the boy into a coughing fit that nearly brings him to his knees. He cups his nose and leans against the sill, glimpsing two cones of light that expose a figure he can only assume is his father. Though the van is nearly invisible, fused as it is with the night, its banshee wail lingers long after it has left the suburbs. The boy listens for signs of his father in the void, and in time is rewarded by the sound of the front door opening. He slinks from his room, marking the time on his bedside clock. Earlier that day, when he had inquired about his father's delayed return, his mother had informed him that there was nothing to worry about, that his father was likely on a learning curve that required a set amount of overtime. *Before you know it, it will be like old times again.* The boy had spent the remainder of the evening in his room, doing his best to concentrate on reading but rarely able to focus, his attention drifting to thoughts of his father's welfare, to a barrage of worse case scenarios. Now, as he situates himself covertly on the top rung of the stairs, the boy glimpses his father standing still as a statue next to the sofa. His mother is at his side, hands raised to his shoulders and whispering something the boy can't make out but that sounds soothing. He slides down a few more rungs, doing his utmost to remain a ghost. His father's suit is wrinkled and soiled, as though it has been exposed to a construction site rather than pristine office space. His face is pale and withdrawn, and he appears on the verge of sleep. While the boy realizes that an intrusion on his part would undoubtedly complicate matters, he can't resist lumbering to the bottom of the stairs with theatrical glee. As he enters the circle of silence surrounding his parents, he wishes he had remained in his hiding place. His father's dead eyes hold him there, as though awaiting direction and, in response, the boy lunges forward to embrace him. After a long delay, the gesture is returned, albeit weakly, hardly comforting. The boy's curiosity can no longer be stilled, his barrage of questions overloud, his need to comprehend taking precedence. Again there is a long delay from his father, who responds with nothing but a paltry pat on the head and a suggestion that they retire to bed. This hardly satisfies the boy, but he nevertheless acquiesces to his mother's suggestion that he return to his room. Once there, he finds it impossible to read, let alone sleep. His only recourse is to sneak back downstairs, place an ear to the closed door of his parents' room, and listen intently for signs of life. In time, he hears his father's familiar snore.

THE BOY CHOKES on fumes in his dream, continuing to do so into wakefulness. His eyes burn, and he struggles to untangle himself from the sheets before shuffling blindly to the window. By the time his senses overcome these morning obstacles, the van and his father are gone, the only evidence being the fresh line of tire tracks next to the previous day's defacement. The boy is disappointed in himself for not rising earlier. He can well imagine his father's heartbreak on discovering the empty second-story window. As he turns, the boy is waylaid by a prolonged coughing fit that coats his palm with an oily layer of phlegm. He shivers and rushes headlong to the bathroom. He places his hand under the faucet, shocked by the residue's resiliency, which clings to his skin like a parasitic caul. In desperation, he scrapes at the gelatinous mass, digging his fingers deep into his skin until the alien thing eventually breaks free and, like a doomed swimmer, swirls down the drain. Relieved, the boy steps into the shower, shifting about under the lukewarm stream. He gargles one scoopful of water after another, but the soreness in his throat does not dissipate. It feels as though an army of ants has collected there. Once he has dressed and slunk down the stairs, he finds his mother in the kitchen, sitting at the polished glass table, a bowl of soggy cereal before her. She is staring at something through the sliding glass door, oblivious of the boy's presence. Instead of preparing his breakfast, the boy turns his attention to a task he knows will make his father proud. Outside, he uncoils the hose and starts spraying the asphalt, methodically working his way down its length. The unsightly van tracks wash away with ease, the muddy remains coursing down the drive like a frothy toxic mass. By the time the boy winds the hose back into its container, the driveway has already begun to dry under the morning sun. Now that its surface has been restored, reality seems a bit more balanced. When the boy returns to the kitchen, fully prepared to join his mother for breakfast, he grows disheartened to discover that the diorama remains unchanged. He pours a bowl of corn flakes and sits in the chair across from his silent mother. Minutes pass before he begins to consume his cereal, which is so mushy that he has to force-finish it, slurping the final dregs in the hope of snapping his mother out of her trance. He waits, growing even more concerned by her inactivity, then takes the bowl to the sink where he meticulously washes it before placing it neatly in the dish rack. He returns to the window in his room to assess his work on the driveway. It appears that he has not done as thorough a job as he had thought. While the dirt has been swept clean, the tracks themselves are still perfectly visible, etched like petroglyphs in stone.

WHEN IT BECOMES obvious that his father won't be returning at the appointed hour, the boy's focus again turns to the driveway. He fills a bucket of soap and water and, with bristle-brush in hand, starts scrubbing the glyphs. It takes more effort than he imagined it would, but with enough elbow grease the patterns do begin to dissipate. It's hot out, the asphalt acting as a conduit, but the boy does not mind. He can douse himself whenever he chooses and it feels good to do so. There is no way he is going to miss the arrival of the van this time, so he is in no rush to finish. He needs a more personal encounter, needs to run a hand across the scabby hide of the monstrosity, get a better view of the parasites within, the things that are feeding on his father. But the wait is long, and the boy grows tired of repeating his task. After spraying the drive a final time, he winds the hose and returns inside. In his room, he sits before his bookcase, withdrawing a paperback he has already read, one of his favorites. He is well into the second chapter when he hears the familiar disturbance outside. He bookmarks his page and races downstairs. By the time he arrives on the front stoop, the van is idling in the middle of the drive. The sun is about to slip away, and the boy wants nothing more than to reel it back, reverse its course, reclaim the degradation done to his father. The van seems perturbed by his presence, unwilling to release his father until he retreats inside. Through the van's darkened windows, the boy registers movement, a shifting of textures. He raises his hand, certain that his father will not only see but be emboldened by the gesture. The van responds with a grotesque squeal, as though to quell the boy's brashness. Emboldened, the boy strides forward, looping around to the van's side. He approaches one of the opaque windows, cups his hand on its surface, and peers inside. His father is lying prone on the floor, surrounded by three individuals in perfectly tailored suits. One of them is pounding the seemingly lifeless chest, as if attempting to revive the man. The boy hammers at the window with equal abandon, quickly gaining the attention of the shadows within. A comical skit of interior commotion ensues, ending with the van's sliding door opening with a violent shriek. The boy retreats a few paces to the border of the drive, and watches as the men exit the van with his father is tow. They move like myriapod across the asphalt, their slicked-back hair and black shoes shined to perfection, components of a collective carapace. The men prop his father in the alcove near the front door and then scuttle back to the van. The sliding door slams shut and the van reverses wildly from the drive and tears off. Only then does the boy retreat to the alcove. The thing that can't possibly be his father is wheezing, struggling for each breath, and all the boy can think to do is sit next to it and clasp its all-too-skeletal hand. As dire as things seem, he remains hopeful that such intimate contact will hasten the thing's recovery, reconstitute the bits that have been siphoned, and return it, in the precious hours that remain before the new workday begins, to the father it once was.

CAMERA OBSCURA

———◆———

HAUGLAND REPOSITIONED THE TRIPOD a few yards downhill, making sure everything was level on the incline before affixing the camera. He took extra care this time around, having nearly dropped the century-old contraption during his last setup. A single dry-plate remained, and if it took extra time for the arrangement, then so be it. He had captured a dozen images of the abandoned farmhouse so far, the production of which had filled the majority of the day, and while at this early stage he could only imagine in his mind's eye the resulting images imprinted upon each plate, he sensed that he had accomplished what he had set out to do. He supposed part of the reason he had spent so much time at this particular location was that today marked the end of the nearly yearlong project he had undertaken to document the abandoned farmsteads of Minnesota. He had chosen to conclude the project in the southeastern corner of the state, mostly because of his genealogical ties to this region, but even more so because of the topography. Since childhood, he had been drawn to this unglaciated wonderland, what with its mysterious back roads, forested hills and, most importantly, hidden farmsteads.

He had collected as much information about each site as local history museums would allow, a bounty of material, the highlights of which he planned to include alongside each photo. So far his editor at the publishing house had been well pleased with the images and text he had shared. For as many house histories as he was able to uncover, there were, unfortunately, a few that had been lost to the vicissitudes of time and decay, remaining anonymous and as derelict as their crumbling structures. Haugland didn't let such uncrackable mystery deter him from photographing a site that appealed to him, as was the case in this final arrangement. When he had initially surveyed the area, using the camera on his phone to document possible sites, the place that left the greatest impression was this one. He had emailed a local historian, attaching images of various farmsteads that he hoped to obtain backstories for, and had been pleasantly surprised by the immediate outpouring of information. His strong familial connection to the area proved of great benefit, and his rapport with the genealogist had grown stronger with each exchange. The woman seemed grateful for his having gotten in touch, and had spent countless hours researching his avalanche of queries. By the time their correspondence came to an end, Haugland felt an even stronger connection to this land of his forebears. The only mystery lay in this final farmstead, the history of which the elder either did not know or was purposefully withholding. All she provided was a last name and a profession: Kolsrud, bachelor farmer. There had to be something she was not telling him, though Haugland was hard-pressed to call her on it because her help up to that point had proven beneficial.

Though he felt deflated by this lack of information regarding the old Kolsrud place, Haugland decided that he would include images of the farmstead anyway, use them for a visual denouement to the book, with the coda that not all mysteries need solving, that mystery was essential to the imagination. Still, Haugland wondered why the old woman had been so tight-lipped. Did she or her family have some connection to certain events that had occurred there? This seemed a possibility, and if so, Haugland need only dig elsewhere to obtain the information. Certainly, others in town could flesh out the history of the place. But he wasn't sure he wanted to dismantle the mystery. At least not yet.

For now, in this bittersweet finale to a project that had consumed so much of his time and energy, Haugland's focus remained only on capturing the best possible image. The lighting was ideal at this hour, and as Haugland tinkered with the final settings and position of the camera, he felt pleasantly overwhelmed by the landscape and the fact that he was on the cusp of finishing his passion project. The camera was ready to go, and Haugland, taking a deep and steady breath, depressed the switch that activated shutter and gears. The intricate internal tick-ticking was music to his ears, and as the century camera made its slow panoramic rotation, he eased himself to the gentle slope of the hill, flattening the tallgrass beneath him. Hands beneath his head, he stared at the cloudless sky and reveled again in his accomplishments. He would spend the weekend obsessively developing the images captured from this final shoot. As hard as it was to admit, he was looking forward to returning to the city after spending so much time in the solitude of the natural world. He had put everything he had into the project, and he knew it would take time to re-regulate himself to life in the real world. Mostly, he would miss these calm moments of communing with nature as the camera did its work. The mechanical whirr, strangely enough, seemed to belong to this environment. If he closed his eyes, Haugland could nearly convince himself that he was listening to the hidden clockwork of the world.

Haugland plucked a length of tallgrass and stuck it between his lips, savoring these final moments. He imagined the details slowly mirroring themselves to the dry-plate. It was a composition of crisp black and white beauty that in many ways was more powerful than the original landscape. Images had the potential of outliving their real-life counterparts, and Haugland's work would be preserved long after the farmhouses deteriorated and became dust. He supposed this was part of the reason he afforded the project with such reverence.

This placid mood was abruptly shattered by an otherworldly and high-pitched scream. It seemed to emanate from the camera and, as Haugland sprang to his feet, the sound was replaced by another he knew too well: the short, sharp shock of cracking glass. The camera continued along its interminably slow rotation, its broken eye already transferring a replica of its jagged wound to the dry-plate. The lens had functioned brilliantly for the entirety of the year, so why it should choose to fail now was beyond comprehension. Haugland voiced his frustration, nearly pushing the tripod over in his rage, but he contained himself enough to allow the camera to finish its course. Perhaps the tainted image would prove interesting and not a total loss. When the ticking gears ceased their full rotation, Haugland carefully detached the camera from the tripod to get a better idea of the extent of the damage. He upended the camera and laid it gently on the flattened spot of tallgrass where he had been resting, then twisted the lens roughly from its wooden housing. A deep fissure bisected the lens, and Haugland felt a crack beginning to develop in him as well. He hoped the incident would not taint the project going forward.

After packing his equipment, Haugland glanced a final time at the old Kolsrud place, a structure that had long enraptured his imagination. He turned his back on it and carefully walked down the hill to the dirt road where he had parked his car. The vehicle's presence, as he homed in on its bright and boxy hull, had him feeling discombobulated, as though he were not perceiving things through his eyes but instead through some past-century relative who could never have been witness to, or understood, such an advancement.

WHILE HAUGLAND HAD INTENDED to begin work in the darkroom on his return, he made the mistake of resting on the sofa before lugging his equipment to the basement. His eyes had grown heavy and the next thing he knew it was half past noon of the following day. As he descended to his workroom through the stairwell—a narrow shaft that was covered with framed photos he considered favorites—Haugland was always left with the impression of moving from one reality to another, which he supposed all creative spaces were designed for. The images on the wall were a visual trigger that shifted his frame of mind. And once he was in the depths of this self-made dream factory, Haugland found it difficult to leave when aboveground responsibilities demanded his attention. It was always disconcerting whenever he had to ascend the stairs and resurface into the current century. Perhaps this was the reason he relied on the photographic techniques used more than a century ago—he was not a man of his time. There had been a period of his creative life when he had fully participated in the digital revolution, producing thousands of photos of the cityscape where he lived, but in the end, the images had left him feeling empty inside. Their sale had provided little else but a stable income, and in time he had begun obsessing to a greater extent about the past, going beyond the simple genealogical concerns that had interested him from an early age. It had taken years of trial and error to feel comfortable with these techniques of the past, but he found that the results were far superior to any image he had ever produced digitally. And he had no intention of yet again allowing the modern to influence and infect him any more than it already had.

The walls of the workroom had once been covered by a excess

of city images, but Haugland had long ago stripped and replaced them with the bulk of his current project. There would be a limit to how many images he could include in the book, and he was still unsure about which ones, in the end, would make the cut. Even the images he considered flawed held a special meaning, resurrecting fond memories of a particular shoot. Some impressions were so powerful that sometimes Haugland felt transported into the landscape, so much so that at times he could nearly feel the heat of the sun or the soft prairie breeze.

Haugland went to the supply counter along the far wall, setting his thermos to the side. He fanned through the selection of vinyl records stacked next to the turntable. Most were composers of Scandinavian origin, and Haugland wavered between Sibelius and Grieg before withdrawing the latter and setting it with utmost care on the turntable. He adjusted the volume and poured himself a cup of coffee. "In the Hall of the Mountain King" put Haugland in the proper mood. After the red lights were lit, his eyes adjusted to the womb-like setting. Such a comparison became even more apt as selected images slowly came into being in the shallow amniotic of the developer. This was magic hour for Haugland and, once he started working, he always had difficulty calling it quits. There was a specialized timer on the counter, but he had purposefully avoided mounting a wall clock. Under the red light, time ceased, and when all was said and done and the space returned to blinding white, Haugland was often surprised by how many hours had passed. The early mornings transitioned in no time to deep night, but fatigue was never a factor and sleep was the furthest thing from his mind. He figured this was due to having spent so much time in the womb, dreaming in his own delectable way, that the real shore of night had no pull. Most evenings he'd be cast adrift, cleaning his cameras for the umpteenth time, perusing his catalog of photos, revising detailed impressions of each, and maybe, if he was lucky, catching an hour or two of sleep at midafternoon of the following day.

Haugland's first image developed beautifully, light and shadow approximating what he had imagined while initially laboring over the shot: a rise in the prairie, the sea of tallgrass arching toward a dilapidated island home. In many ways, the image drew all the important details out of the physical setting, captured the character of its soul. The black and white composition lent an air of mystery, stripped away reality's harsh glare. Like an alchemist, Haugland could manipulate the scene even further, if he so wished, heightening its emotions through experimentation. This first photo seemed to him as close to perfection as he could hope for. Usually, he nitpicked images as they went through processing, but as he pulled this one from the fix and clipped it to the drying rack, its beauty overwhelmed him. It was only as he was turning away to begin work on the second exposure that he noticed a small blemish on the print. A shadowy presence, for lack of a better term, stood beyond the broken porch, and for the life of him, he could not shake the idea that he had captured some ghostly resident standing before its domain. No, the only logical explanation was that the blemish was of soil that had adhered to the lens. It did not lessen the impact of the image, and in a sense added intrigue. The presence was blurred and ethereal, giving the impression of a ghost caught in a haunted landscape. Haugland would crop and enlarge the image later on, after making initial prints of the other images. He wondered if he would be able to draw out more detail, or if the blemish would collapse on itself.

These suppositions were thrown to the wayside when he developed the second, third, and fourth images. Each contained the self-same blemish, though not in the exact position as the first. The shift in the second photograph was hardly discernible, and Haugland had to carefully compare the new image against the first to realize that, yes, there had been movement, accompanied by what appeared to be a raising of one hand, as though the specter were attempting to gain Haugland's attention. In the third shot the willowy defect moved closer still and, unbelievably, became more defined. When Haugland closed his eyes, his mind's eye fleshed the ghostly imperfection into a long-haired young woman, her sharp nose and round chin suggesting a poetic litheness. All was not lost when he opened his eyes, for the fantasy behind his lids seemed to resolve the flaw even further, leaving Haugland embarrassed by a sexual reverie that spoke volumes to his current companionless state. Indeed, if he remembered back to the last fling he had had—one he had hoped would develop into a more lasting relationship—the individual in question greatly resembled this specter. And while his initial reaction had been one of dismay, he grew to appreciate the unexpected and beautiful detail, imagining that the series of ghostly photos might be unified into another smaller-scaled project. Gears were already turning as to how he might pitch the idea to his editor.

While the specter continued to creep closer in subsequent images, it was only when Haugland examined the tenth that a strange new detail emerged. Nothing yet had come into true focus—all the result of the subject's continual movement. This was part of the charm of using the old technique. Exposure time was slower than modern film, which could capture most movement with crystal clarity. In this instance, the subject's long hair and what appeared to be a flowing white gown was accompanied by a ghostly trail of smoke that seemed to emanate from her lower back and curl downward around her leg like a spectral tail. Haugland didn't think too much of this at first, figuring it was no more than a portion of the prairie grass she was wading through, but when it came into greater focus in subsequent images, Haugland could not escape the impression that this wispy appendage was an essential part of the individual in question. And so the project shifted again, this time following a more folkloric route. Its focus would be on the *huldra*, that enthralling creature of Norse myth.

As Haugland continued to develop the final images, he focused less and less on the Kolsrud place and more on the mysterious figure as it continued its slow approach. By the third to last image, facial details were beginning to emerge, and by the penultimate Haugland's heart was racing. The Kolsrud place was nowhere to be seen, the entirety of the frame having been permeated by the face of the so-called specter, a face of ethereal beauty. The print was so detailed that Haugland half expected the subject to part her lips in either pleasantry or kiss. All through the development process, Haugland could not take his eyes from the image. Hours might have passed for all he knew or cared. It was the most beautiful photo he had ever captured, and it took him an eternity to draw his attention away and realize that a final image still needed to be developed.

The resulting photo turned out to be the antipode of the previous. As the picture drew into focus in the developer tray, Haugland recalled the moment the century camera's lens had cracked. The shock he had experienced then was replicated now as he gazed in semi-horror at another portrait, this one cracked and blemished beyond all reason, shattering the woman's previous beauty and revealing a bark-like decay beneath the surface. Haugland wondered if this was merely the result of the cracked lens, or if the transformation had occurred within the figure itself. Of all the wondrous images he had captured during his last shoot, this alone was the one Haugland felt no compulsion to keep. He halted the process at the developer and tossed the grotesquerie into the trash.

He made quick work of cleaning up, and by the time he withdrew from the red-light womb and collected the images from the drying rack, he was already well on his way to forgetting about the final portrait. The undeniable beauty of the second to last image made sure of that.

TWO DAYS LATER, Haugland retraced his route to the Kolsrud place. The drive was exhausting. He supposed this was due to his obsessive work schedule, but the overcast sky was also to blame. After fifty miles he had nearly called it quits and returned home, wishing he had checked the weather forecast before venturing out. Not that he couldn't capture some gloomy black and white imagery along the way—though, to be honest, he wasn't in the mood. What pushed him forward was a new obsession: unveiling a mystery.

The portrait of the woman would not leave him. He had fashioned hundreds of prints of her in various modes, experimenting with the image to stunning effect. He had enjoyed immersing himself in each incarnation, and had he been able to sink bodily into the development process, he would have done so, becoming one with this mysterious madonna. All fantasies considered, the only realistic option was a return to the source of origin—though even this seemed an impulsive act, a foundation sure to crumble under false reverie.

Haugland was feeling worse for wear by the time he pulled to the edge of the country road next to the Kolsrud place. He stepped from the car, his legs stiff and his back aching. He withdrew his gear from the back seat, and trudged through the tallgrass that covered the hill. The weather had lost some of its gloominess. Haugland just hoped that it would cooperate enough for him to capture a few more images, to lure mystery out of hiding. He planted the tripod in the same spot as before, and while his first impulse was to rush through the process of set-up, he did his level best to put as much care into his efforts as he ever had. By the time he had attached the camera to the base of the tripod, adjusted the new lens, and inserted the first slide of film, he felt confident that he had exactly replicated the conditions of his previous shoot.

Haugland's first order of business was to investigate the house, with his digital camera in tow, documenting its dilapidation and with luck capturing an image or two of its ethereal occupant. Idle curiosity led him to frame his first image directly in front of the tripod, merely to ascertain if the newfangled camera was able to detect things unseen. After the photo had been stored to internal memory, Haugland viewed it through the digital display, noticing nothing out of the ordinary. He dove deeper into the image, zooming as far as he could to the area beyond the porch, to the place where he had first glimpsed the ghostly imperfection. The clarity of the image was impeccable but revealed nothing beyond what was already there. He shifted the image vector, examining various other quadrants of the house, with special focus on the windows, most of which had been stripped of glass. He lingered on one of the upper windows, trying to determine if the shadow he detected there contained enough detail to suggest the human form or was merely an oddly hanging drape. He sensed that his imagination was getting the better of him, so he shouldered his camera and started toward the house. The sky was relatively free of clouds, and his intuition told him that he would have plenty of time to complete his work. Halfway to the house, he turned and took a photo of the old camera. It rose like a buoy in the deep sea of the prairie.

When Haugland reached the porch, he found the spot where the blurred figure had first appeared. He half expected to experience a chill, but the space didn't seem to hold any spectral residue. He stepped onto the porch, which creaked beneath his weight, and took a series of close-ups of the disintegrating railing. Its textures of peeling paint contained an abstract beauty that Haugland could not resist. He turned his attention to the warped window next to the door, capturing in its reflection a brightly lit but distorted prairie. Even the tripod could be seen, its blurred outline resembling an interloper. By the time he stepped into the house, Haugland had taken nearly fifty images.

The interior resembled many of the other locations he'd taken the opportunity to walk through, its floors strewn with all manner of dusty detritus. As much as the porch had drawn his artistic eye, he knew that this space would absorb even more. So much vied for his attention that he had a difficult time deciding where to begin. He decided to wander a bit more, heading for the stairs and the second floor. The stairs creaked and shifted beneath his feet, causing him more than a little trepidation. The rail was so wobbly that after one touch Haugland decided to avoid it altogether.

By the time he arrived on the second level, the interior had darkened a discernible degree. He walked to the window overlooking the front of the house, and peered into the distant prairie. The wind had picked up. He could hear it whistling through the broken ruin. Tallgrass swayed to and fro, and a gust of wind was strong enough to uproot the tripod and send it to the ground. The prairie seemed alive, its vast, undulating maw working to remove all evidence of his visit. Haugland scanned the area and could not even see his vehicle or the road beneath the rise. Without such anchors, he felt dislocated. A heavy downpour followed, obscuring and further transforming his view. He listened to the wind blasting through the reed-like apertures of the house, and it too seemed to change, altering from intonations evoking terror into something more pleasing to his ears, something like singing.

Haugland retreated from the window, determined to get out of the house and retrieve his rain-soaked equipment before the storm got worse. This might be the final force of nature to topple the century-old abode. Haugland descended the stairs, feeling more exhausted with each step. It took his every effort not to stumble and fall. At the bottom of the stairs, the windsong intensified. It was comforting, bringing a moody solace similar to Sibelius or Grieg. Haugland shifted along the wall and shuffled through the main room to the front door beyond. From there he had a direct view outside, though most of the landscape was obscured by a woman standing in profile on the porch. She seemed to be singing to the prairie.

Haugland stared at the bark-like skin of the woman's lower back and at the obscene swirl of what appeared to be a tail. She turned toward him and made her way nakedly into her domain, continuing to sing. Her tail flicked playfully to either side of her hips, and her seductive lips were parted in a sinister smile. Had Haugland been able move, he would have met her halfway, but he felt as inert as his century camera. His eyes were the lens that captured everything on the dry-plate of his mind.

The woman's appearance changed as she strode across the detritus of the floor, so that by the time she was midway to Haugland, her arms and abdomen and nearly the entirety of her neck and face had transitioned from pearlescent to a putrid, bark-like flesh. And her song remained as beautiful as ever. Haugland focused on it even as the spindly-limbed creature embraced him like a long-lost lover who had finally returned home. Her transition—like an exposure gone wrong—was so overpowering that Haugland would have given anything to close his eyes. But such an act was lost to him. As the final, horrific exposure coalesced in his mind, he fell to his knees and became one with the detritus.

And all the while his obsession continued its ancient and all-consuming song.

DESCRAMBLER

———— ◆ ————

For David Cronenberg

MAX HEARD THE VAN well in advance of it turning onto his street. Its droning exhaust was like the theme to some mythic grade-Z video. Clamshell-encased cassettes in hand, Max wended his way through the hoard that his mother had made of their home during his father's long and likely permanent absence. Once outside, he strode through the cluttered lawn to the weed-blighted boulevard where he awaited the arrival of the video dealer.

In time, Ryshpan's van lumbered around the bend and crept to the curb. It idled there, engine ticking, ruined exhaust fouling the air. An off-center logo filled the upper quadrant of the sliding door, with RYSHPAN VIDEO crammed into a space trying its best to resemble a VHS tape. Max had never asked, but he assumed the design was the video dealer's handiwork. Crude as it was, Max loved every inch of it.

The sliding door unlocked, popping from its seal like a pressurized lid. As the panel clattered along a corroded, chain-driven track, Max moved closer to the illuminated interior. A wire display rack spanned the length of the far wall, each row filled with video-cassettes held in place by frayed bungee cords. The majority of Ryshpan's merchandise, however, resided in genre-labeled plastic bins situated along the floor of the gutted van.

To Max, the organized chaos of this mobile video outlet contained a charm and comfort he could not fully express. He deposited his returns into the bin housed in the space that had once contained a passenger seat. Ryshpan, already half-turned in the driver's seat, offered his standard silent greeting. His smile was as broad and fixed as the Cheshire Cat. Dark-framed glasses, containing the thickest lenses Max had ever seen, refashioned the video dealer's eyes into shifting peppercorns, and his shock of wavy auburn hair seemed to move of its own accord in the breezeless space.

"Enjoy the flicks this week?" Ryshpan asked.

Max nodded and turned his attention to the bungee-restrained wall of cassettes. Taken collectively, their covers represented the most darkly exquisite mural Max had ever laid eyes on. His dream was to someday fashion a similar mural on one of the walls of his room, if and when he acquired enough cassettes to do so.

"*Network of Blood* was cool," he said, lifting a cassette from the bin labeled BODY HORROR. "Got anything else by the director?" Max bent deeper into the van and selected two additional clam-shelled horrors from the wall.

"You're in luck," Ryshpan said, leaning toward the glove compartment. The darkened, rectangular space resembled the front of a VCR, from which the video dealer withdrew a cassette. "Here's his latest." He held the tape aloft with reverence. "This one's special."

Max hesitated but eventually grabbed the cassette. He then turned his attention to another bin, where he made his final selection: *Tales From the Quadead Zone*. He reached into his pocket, withdrew a few crumpled bills, and deposited them into the burlap sack affixed to the side of Ryshpan's seat.

"Don't forget your magazine," the video dealer said, his arm resting casually on the dash, finger ready to depress the custom-made switch that activated the sliding door.

Max reached into the cardboard box next to the returns bin and withdrew a back issue of *Fangoria* with Pinhead gracing its cover. He gazed at the lurid details for too long, forgetting about the sliding door. It was on the verge of pinning him to the threshold before he leaped back.

"Until next week, my friend," Ryshpan said before the door locked in place.

The van slammed into gear and lumbered down the street, its damaged soundtrack accompanying Max to his room, where it eventually faded to black.

MAX'S INITIAL ENCOUNTER with the video dealer had been outside the local Blockbuster. The van had shown up two months ago, idling defiantly in the parking lot as Max exited the store with his bag of videos. The logo on the van drew his attention, and, after yanking his Kuwahara from the steel corral, he wheeled in for a closer look. Ryshpan grinned from the open window, elbows resting on the sill, a tattered clipboard in hand.

"First week of seven is free," he proclaimed, tossing the clipboard near the balding front tire of the Kuwahara. Dumbfounded, Max bent to retrieve it, scanning the names and addresses that filled its sheets. He recognized a few on the list, mostly classmates from school.

As much as he wanted to subscribe, Max returned the clipboard that night and pedaled casually from the parking lot, looking over his shoulder more times than he cared to admit. Two weeks later, after having grown weary of Blockbuster's popular and predictable fare, he again approached the van, setting his apprehension aside to add his name and address to the list. The idea of a mobile video store appealed to him on so many levels, and he was excited to begin this new phase of his video existence.

Before Max ventured home, Ryshpan gifted him his first complimentary back issue of *Fangoria*.

IN HIS ROOM, Max had a closer look at the mystery cassette. The majority of the video dealer's stock was protected by clamshell casings that were near at the end of their life cycle. But not this one. There were no identifying labels, and its overall pristine condition had Max wondering if it was a blank cassette. The longer he held it, the more he realized that its texture seemed off, as though it had been produced using a material other than plastic. It felt nearly as pliant as the grips of his Kuwahara.

Max squeezed another cassette from its case and held the pair beneath the ceiling light, searching for textural differences. His mind had obviously been playing tricks, for they looked and felt like any other mass-produced VHS. He knocked the cassettes together, their inner spools clattering familiarly, then inserted the unmarked one into the VCR. As internal mechanisms whirred, Max retreated to the edge of his bed. Static-infused darkness infested the TV screen, the image rippling for half a minute before transitioning to a full-on stream of static. Max waited for the opening credits, but nothing came. He rose to eject the tape, wondering why Ryshpan had deceived him in such a way.

Midway to the TV, he stopped. The screen was expanding exponentially as if the static-stream could no longer be contained within its plastic reservoir. It continued to swell, the accompanying audio growing in intensity like a swarm of gnats. Max was paralyzed in disbelief, mesmerized by the . . . hallucination? He wondered if he dare step into its midst to hit the STOP button, but by the time the decision was made the impossible swarm had eclipsed the whole of the VCR and was now advancing toward him like industrial smoke. The mass curled when it met the floor and ceiling, and as it advanced across the latter, Max backstepped until he lost his equilibrium and spilled onto the bed. As though sensing his vulnerability, the static rained down like particles drawn to a magnet.

Max felt them searing into his skin as he lost consciousness.

WHEN HE CAME TO, it felt as though little time had passed. The only difference was that the impossible swarm no longer dominated his room. He rose from his bed, arms outstretched with typical early-morning exhaustion, feeling as though he'd experienced a full night's sleep. His clock told otherwise. Only ninety minutes had passed. He surveyed his room, expecting to find lingering traces of static. But everything looked normal. The TV was on, its bright blue screen putting Max on edge as he imagined it filling the room with another illusion.

He cautiously approached the VCR and, with a trembling finger, tapped the EJECT button. After an interminable wait, the machine spat out the cassette. Max yanked it from the slot and peered at the inner spool, surprised to find it had played out in its entirety. More than likely the run-time had been ninety minutes, the same span he'd been out. At his desk, he slipped the cassette under the stack of those he had yet to view and grabbed the topmost clamshell. He pinched its lower quadrant and jerked the cassette free, feeling a sense of normalcy return. It was nearly midnight, but Max wasn't tired in the least. Maybe viewing another video would help.

He inserted *Tales From the Quadead Zone*, turned off the overhead light, and slipped into bed. The TV blipped from black to an explosion of static, remaining in this state for longer than it should have. Max tore the bedspread aside and lunged for the STOP button, not wishing to repeat his earlier experience. So far, the static remained contained, cordoned off by the thick plastic walls of the

TV. Nevertheless, Max did not hesitate to eject the cassette and try another video.

Each of the seven turned out to be defective, containing nothing but bands of static. Curious, Max checked a few of the tapes in his library—and was met with the same result. Every VHS in his possession had been infected by Ryshpan's viral video. As disheartening and devastating as this was, Max knew he needed to get some sleep. Instead of doing so, he located his back issues of *Fangoria* from beneath the bed and curled up to read.

In the silence of the room, the sound of static echoed in his ears.

NOTHING WAS RIGHT the following morning. To Max, it appeared as if reality was double-exposed, though not in the sense of familiar objects being duplicated. Instead, there seemed to be an overlay of sorts, one that grew more prominent with each passing hour.

How he made it through the school day was beyond him. The ride home had seen him hiding in the rear seat of the bus, eyes closed for the majority of the ride. Horrors existed here as well, though not to the extent of what he had witnessed on the streets of his hometown. The scuttling skinless things appeared vaguely humanoid, but only in the manner of their head, torso, and limbs. Their long, emaciated appendages and distended bellies spoke of perpetual starvation, and their movement was most frantic when they drew near unsuspecting townsfolk going about their daily business. As they circled certain individuals, these monstrosities would thrust their elongated heads mongrel-like to the ground, seeming to feast on something Max could not readily see.

When he could no longer stomach the sight outside, Max shifted his attention to the interior of the bus. From the center aisle, one of the eyeless things was observing him. Its long desiccated fingers clasped the edge of the vinyl seat, and it "looked" at him with what felt like clinical detachment. Its nose, which now existed as a hollow cavity, sniffed at the air, and what appeared to be its mouth opened as though on the verge of communication. As the lips parted, however, the toothless maw produced no words. Instead, a thin tongue curled outward from the lipless mouth and seemed to test the air. The creature dipped its head to the seat and shifted uncomfortably close, forcing Max to retreat as far as he could, until the cold metal of the bus gouged his side. The creature worked frantically, silently, and Max felt trapped. The only sound, besides chattering classmates, was the diesel-rumbling of the bus.

Eventually, the thing completed its weird feast, drifting back to a more observational stance. There was an intelligence there, and it was easy for Max to imagine that in some prior life this monster had been human. As the mouth appendage slowly retracted into its parched lips, Max noticed all the dust still collected about its mouth.

More than anything, Max wished he had his wrist-rocket. That could do some damage at this close range. He reached out a trembling hand, wanting to determine the corporality of the thing or if it was mere illusion. Before he could make contact, the creature disappeared down the aisle, the fast-forward motion reminiscent of a VCR tuned exclusively to the thing itself.

WHATEVER THE THINGS were—Max's only theory was that their population consisted of the long-dead residing in some purgatorial overlay, their only means of contact with this world being the dust it produced. *Bottom Feeders From the Fifth Dimension*—this struck Max as the perfect title for a film, and he grew excited by the possibilities. In the last year he'd been drawn to the idea of filmmaking, and maybe this Z-grade experience would inspire him to begin his journey. He could even get Ryshpan involved, distributing the film to the underground market. Further inspired, Max braved the depths of the basement to find the high-end "cat's-eye" camcorder his father had left behind. As Max loaded the machine with a blank cassette, he imagined some future interview with *Fangoria* where the question of origins was posed: "Tell us more about the inspiration behind your award-winning debut?"

Max had not crossed paths with any more of the Feeders since returning from school. Nevertheless, he had gone through each room with his wrist-rocket and a few marbles from the jar on his desk. He wanted to make sure none of the Feeders were hiding in any of the dusty corners of the house. When his mother asked what he was doing, he continued his search without a word, and before long she went back to watching her show. She was used to him roaming about the house in such a state, his quirky imagination leading the way.

Max eventually retreated to his room and charged the camcorder for half an hour before venturing outside, hopeful that he might capture one of the Feeders on tape. He could either use the footage in *Bottom Feeders* or turn it over to the local media. Would they believe such evidence, or tag it as an elaborate hoax? Obviously the latter. Max wandered for six blocks, encountering dozens of people—none of whom were accompanied by the parasites. His reality, it seemed, had been cleansed. But for how long?

Max was eager to question Ryshpan about the time-released delusion he had undergone. Was it some new manner of immersive technology that the video dealer had been paid to test on unsuspecting patrons? Had exposure to the mystery tape really allowed Max to glimpse into another dimension normally not visible to the naked eye, or had it all been his imagination?

Later that evening, Max had his answer. After inserting one of Ryshpan's cassettes, fully expecting to encounter the same static-filled erasure, he instead sat on the edge of his bed and watched the movie play through its designated run-time, unblemished and picture-perfect. Encouraged, he viewed each rental in turn, savoring every minute.

It was nearly three a.m. when he finished, and as much as he wanted to give the mystery cassette another try, he held off—and continued to do so for the entirety of the week.

Until Ryshpan's return.

STACK OF CLAMSHELLS in hand, Max scanned the area as though expecting to encounter a stray Feeder or two. But the neighbor-

hood was as quiet and unassuming as it had ever been. In time—
right on time—Ryshpan's van pulled to the curb, its sliding door
retracting like a beetle's elytra before flight. As usual, the video
dealer was half turned in his seat, showcasing his all-consuming
smile and bespectacled eyes.

"So, what's the verdict? Pretty trippy, right?"

Max stared at the video dealer, dropping his returns into the bin
without saying a word. Ryshpan reached toward the glove compartment and withdrew another cassette. He held it out to Max.

"I guarantee you'll like this one even better," he said.

Max eyed the cassette and considered taking it, but in the end
declined the offer, selecting seven standard videos from the bins.
He wasn't sure he was ready to experience another experimental
format, at least not this week. And besides, he had more than enough
inspiration to begin early production work on *Bottom Feeders*. He
planned to start the script tonight on his mother's old Olivetti, a
machine that, once his fingers began depressing keys, never failed
to remind him of a clattering bug.

"Your loss, my friend," Ryshpan said after Max paid for his
rentals. "This is the future. Total immersion, and that ain't the
half of it . . . this new stuff'll blow your mind."

As the door slid shut, Max could still hear the video dealer's
voice going on and on about the future of video, but it was so
layered with static that he could not make out the words. The van
pulled away, its hull and the reality around it glitching like the
blemished image on an overplayed VHS tape.

This visual glitch occurred twice more as Max returned to his room—once while reaching for the front door, and the other after glimpsing his mother in her TV chair—but in the end, the reality of things tracked back into focus and continued to play along its eternal plastic spool.

THE IN-BETWEEN

———— ◆ ————

TIM PULLED TO THE CURB in front of his childhood home, his attention drawn to the squat, brown-trimmed rambler he had spent his formative years in. He was uncertain as to how many owners had come and gone during his twenty-year absence, but it was clear that none of them had applied any exterior change. The only shock was in how diminutive everything looked. Viewed through the lens of youth, the house and environs had always seemed so palatial. And while it wasn't exactly nostalgia that had brought Tim here, he basked in it now because he didn't know how any of what he had planned would play out.

It had taken a certain amount of willpower for Tim to revisit these suburbs, and he had nearly bypassed it all. Even now it felt as though a part of him had remained on the highway and was already spectrally retracing his route home. It would have been easier to have done so, but thoughts of Eric steadied his resolve.

51

Even after all these years, there was not a day that went by that he did not think of his childhood friend and the circumstances of his disappearance. Tim knew exactly where Eric had gone, but no one in the neighborhood, not even his parents, had believed him. His tear-laden report had been the stuff of childhood fantasy. Eric's always-stern parents had accused Tim of not keeping track of their son, and continued blaming him in an indirect way for years afterward. Tim thought he had put everything behind him and come to terms with Eric's "abduction," which was how the rest of the town defined the disappearance. He had been lured, they said, into a stranger's vehicle and, with no witnesses present, vanished without a trace. As Tim drifted into nostalgic-minded middle age, he had felt an overwhelming compulsion to revisit the disappearance with a keener and more worldly eye.

He stepped from his car, purposefully steering his attention away from the forested land that lay directly across the street. It had been dubbed The In-between by the boys in the neighborhood, mostly because it was the only plot of land that had escaped development. Houses had been erected to either side, but for some reason developers had chosen to ignore this patch of real estate. Even now it was impossible for Tim not to feel its pull, but he kept his focus on his childhood home—and on the possibility of meeting the current owner, having a quick peek inside. As he strode along the concrete path that led to the front door, he was surprised by all the cracks and sprouting weeds. His father had always been so meticulous about such things. He never would have allowed it to get so bad.

Tim need not have worried about an invitation to enter, however, for when he arrived at the threshold his attention was drawn to a sun-bleached CONDEMNED sign. He stared at it in disbelief and thought he heard laughter in the wind. The In-between hadn't forgotten how to taunt him. Tim took a deep breath and turned to sit on the concrete stairs. He stared at the unkempt pathway, feeling defeated under a sky that seemed to have darkened. Memories of Eric crowded his thoughts. When they became too much, he reluctantly lifted his gaze and stared at that once majestic place where he and his friends had fashioned so many memories.

For years it had been their playground, and none of them had ever once thought to question why the area had been allowed to grow wild. It merely *was*, and for that they were daily grateful. To have such a unique stomping grounds so close to home was a boon to the boredom of their treeless and always trimmed backyards. More importantly, it allowed them to escape the prying eyes of their parents. It was a spot where their secrets remained secure, where their imaginations ruled the day. It wasn't until years later, when Tim and his family had moved from the neighborhood to the other side of town, that he came to understand the corrupting nature of The In-between. It had affected each boy differently, but back then none of them, not even Tim, had understood how far the deception had gone. At the time, in their view, The In-between was the holiest of sanctuaries. They used it, it did not use them.

Now, as Tim's attention drifted over its shadow-dappled surface, he thought he could detect hundreds of sinister smiles embedded in its tightly-knit wall of green. In the breezeless afternoon, the monstrosity seemed to undulate, as though seeking to unmoor and crawl nearer his position. Tim shook his head. His imagination was as potent as it had been twenty years ago. The longer he sat idle with his thoughts, the easier it would be to just up and leave. And if it came to that, he knew he'd never have the courage to return to this place, saturated as it was with so much dread.

Tim broke from his paralysis and stood. Before he could take his first step, however, he heard a vehicle approaching from the same direction that he had come. It crawled along at a leisurely pace, slower than was necessary, as though the driver had also come here under the influence of nostalgia and was attempting to take in as much of the neighborhood as possible. The vehicle was a wood-paneled station wagon of a vintage that had been popular during Tim's adolescence. This one was rusted beyond all possible restoration, its faux wood panels sun-faded and peeling. As it passed by, Tim could not see the driver, but in the back window a young boy's face was pressed like a suckling amoeba against the glass. Tim began to panic until he realized it was all for show, that the young passenger was not an abductee screaming for help, not already-lost Eric being led into the great unknown.

Tim watched as the car turned into the driveway of the house adjacent to The In-between. He tried to remember the name of the boy who had lived there, but his memory kept misfiring. As he waited for the specifics to return, he focused more intently on the station wagon. It idled a few feet from the garage, as though waiting for the door to open on its own accord. The door was askew, so that when it did begin to move, its pace was cartoonishly slow. It would raise a foot, hesitate, drop an inch, hesitate, ratchet up another foot, hesitate, and so on. Tim mentally willed the door to its apex, because the longer the farce went on, the more tense he became—as though the outcome had some bearing on his own success or failure.

When the door finally locked in place, a cloud of oil smoke exploded from the rear of the station wagon. The squealing vehicle then lurched into the garage, and Tim half expected it to utter a final, wailing plea before its connecting parts failed. He waited in anticipation for the driver to exit, sensing intuitively that this was one of his boyhood friends grown to adulthood. The car continued to idle, and it did not take long for its exhaust to fill the small space with black fog. As the garage door closed, Tim grew concerned about the safety of the driver and, more importantly, the child. He was on the verge of rising from the stoop, fully prepared to light out across the street, when he noticed the curtains in the bay window part to reveal a middle-aged man. His bald head, jaundiced skin, and lifeless eyes were reminiscent of a cancer victim. Tim lifted a hand in acknowledgment, expecting a return gesture, but the man did no more than stare before receding into darkness. The creepy stillness of this old neighborhood spoke of an inevitable demise, one that Tim had a hard time accepting. People did tend to stick to themselves these days, but everything in that regard seemed all the more heightened here. His beloved neighborhood had turned into a dark comedy. The only feature of it that had remained vibrant and unchanged was The In-between.

Tim detected movement in his periphery and turned to see a young boy gliding down the street. He was on a bicycle similar in style to the one he had once owned, its elongated chrome handlebars and banana seat making him nearly swoon with excitement. The boy came to a skidding halt in front of The In-between. He looked pale and his mullet-style haircut seemed more wig than growth. Tim nearly called out to him, wanting to ask a few general questions about the neighborhood, but instead he watched as the boy pulled his bike over the curb and, without preamble, strode toward the wall of green.

A minute later, Tim noticed two other boys on bikes pedaling furiously toward the same spot. He wondered if they were attempting to catch up with their companion or trying to prevent him from entering the woods. It was also possible that they were the local bully squad out for blood. Their pallor was similar to that of the leader of the pack, and they sported the same false-looking mullet. After they deposited their bikes, one of them stumbled on his shoelaces and was thrown violently to the ground. His arms shot out to break the fall, but momentum sent his hair flying. He rose to his feet, brushing himself off before bending to retrieve the accouterment. Instead of reaffixing the wig to his bald pate, he tucked the mass beneath his belt as though it were the pelt of his most recent kill. He then tore through the opening in the woods, his companion following close behind.

The entrance to The In-between was child-sized, and Tim had never thought of it in terms of a maw until now. The longer he stared at the undulating curtain of green, the easier it was to reconsider his plan. He stood up and began walking toward the car. When he arrived, he felt at a crossroads. It would be so easy to just drive away, forget about everything. He tapped his trouser pocket, to ensure that the lighter was still there, then opened the passenger-side door to retrieve the can of gas on the floorboard. Fumes had accumulated in the enclosed space, and after setting the can near the curb, Tim went around the car to roll down each window. It would be aired out by the time he completed his task in the woods.

Tim picked up the can and looked before crossing the street, feeling more than ever like a little kid again. He walked to the abandoned bicycles, their chrome hulls like lures meant to draw his attention. As he squatted next to one, he was shocked to discover all the rust that had collected on its surface, as though it had been abandoned years, not minutes, ago. Weeds and grass poked through its spokes, and the bicycle itself seemed fused to the ground.

Dumfounded, Tim rose to his feet and surveyed the surface of The In-between. Unlike the diminutive-seeming nature of his childhood home, the woods struck him as even more immense than he remembered. It felt as though he was standing in front of a vast, static sea wave that might at any moment crash onto him. He grew despondent thinking about this and the bikes and all the eroded architecture of his old neighborhood—a place that he had always thought was timeless. The In-between alone had retained vitality, as if it were a parasite slowly draining its hosts dry. Tim wondered if the neighborhood would heal once the woods were expunged.

He took his first tentative step through the entrance, and was nearly past the threshold when he felt an urgent tug to his right hand—the one that held the gas can. He glanced back, startled to find that his arm had become entangled in a conglomeration of branches. Pain encircled his wrist, followed by a tightening sensation that had him nearly dropping the gas can. He cried out in pain as he attempted to yank free, putting all his weight behind the effort. The vines binding his wrist snapped so unexpectedly that Tim was sent sprawling to the forest floor. He pushed himself up, pleased to discover that he still had the gas can.

Tim spotted the main footpath that bisected the whole of The In-between. He had walked this path so many times, leading or following his friends, the lot of them pretending that they were marching over the exposed spine of some great buried beast. Tim thought again of the mullet-haired boys, and while he was still convinced that they had been a delusion, he kept his ears peeled for sounds of movement, for snapping twigs or conspiratorial whispers behind trees. The stillness of the place was overwhelming, but he pushed past his fear and followed the footpath, silently counting his steps, knowing exactly how many he would need to take before he arrived at the heart of this unhallowed place. And it was there that he planned to burn it from the inside out.

The woods hadn't changed much since his last visit, which was strange given that over twenty years had passed. He and his friends had spent countless hours wandering its depths, a place that seemed to expand or contract depending on one's mood. The boys had built numerous makeshift shelters during the years, most of which were composed of debris found within its boundaries. Occasionally, one of them would introduce an item from beyond its borders, a hubcap found along the curb, a tattered flag pulled from a garbage bin, wind chimes stolen from a neighbor's yard. They hadn't realized it, but they were building a small woodland community, complete with carefully-trod pathways.

Tim hadn't been the one to discover the stone foundation, but he'd been the first to arrive after hearing Eric's call. His friend had been digging out a section of earth, with the plan of erecting a fire pit, when his shovel had clattered against stone. When Tim arrived, Eric was down on his hands and knees brushing away as much soil from the stone's surface as he could. It was clear that what he had found was not a boulder but instead a stone block that was at least two feet wide. As Eric continued to peel away layers of soil, it became evident that a series of these blocks had been abutted next to one another. When the other boys arrived, Tim and the rest of them took turns with the shovel, uncovering as much of the foundation as they could before exhaustion and the setting sun had sent them home.

The discovery of the stone foundation shifted the group's focus from construction to obsessive excavation. Each had their theory of what it was they were unearthing, but Eric's contribution was the best. He imagined that the foundation was part of some ancient structure erected long before the arrival of European settlers and predating Indigenous peoples themselves. The possibility of such antiquity had sent Tim scurrying to the library the following day, loading his backpack with books containing images of various ancient edifices. He had always had a strong artistic talent, and he spent hours of his free time sketching out a variety of possibilities as to how the structure might have looked.

But it all turned out to be wrong. What they had thought was a foundation was instead the apex of the structure. This revelation did not deter the boys in the least. They were more than happy to continue with the excavation. Tim was the only exception, having grown tired of slaving away, and wanting nothing more than to get back to the building and exploring that had previously filled their afternoons. When Eric and the rest of them started digging even deeper along the sides of the structure, Tim had stormed home and sat despondently on his front stoop. He had waited there for nearly an hour, expecting as each minute passed that his friends would follow suit.

Tim reluctantly returned the following day, mostly to try to steer his friends away from the dig, suggesting several options that had enticed them in the past: a bike ride to Silver Lake, a walk to Les's Superette, a matinee at the Plaza theater. The boys listened to his every word, but their expressions remained blank. Eric spoke next, with a reverence that made his face glow, stating that the work they were doing was important, and that nothing in their lives was more pressing. Tim hadn't planned to help, but in the end, he picked up a shovel and worked alongside his friends. Not only that day, but the next, and the next. And as their commitment to the excavation grew, obligations such as school and church and family became unbearable. They were working themselves to death, though none except Tim would ever admitted to this.

And then Eric vanished—abducted, according to the authorities. The disappearance hadn't fazed the remaining boys, who continued to show up at the dig site with blind determination. Tim, on the other hand, was devastated. He spent weeks away from The In-between, holed up in his room trying to come to terms with Eric's disappearance, but in time the welfare of his friends lured him back, where he did his best to convince them to stop. But the harder he pushed, the more resistant they became. An undeniable compulsion was visible in their glassy eyes, and Tim wondered why he alone was immune to the influence that had so strongly taken hold of his friends.

He longed for a return to that time before the discovery, so much so that when he showed up at the site one morning in late summer, he was not able to contain his emotions. He lit into his friends with a tirade that shocked even himself, tossing his shovel onto the blasted heath, cursing it, proclaiming that its discovery was the worst thing to have ever happened to him and them. His friends did nothing but stare at him, not in disbelief, but as though he was a hindrance to the work. Tim retreated from the encroaching confines of the woods, pushing through branches and kicking at bushes and brambles until he was on the other side. He mounted his bicycle, stared at The In-between, and silently cursed its existence. He felt such a sense of loss. At home, he gazed from his bedroom window, watching the woods and waiting for his friends to appear. And in time they did, their exhausted bodies mounting their bicycles and pedaling for home. From that moment on, Tim longed for his family to move, if not out of the neighborhood at least to the end of it, so that he wouldn't have to be reminded of his loss.

As it turned out, he remained in proximity to The In-between for many years to come. And the more he ignored it during his waking hours, the more it menaced his dreams. He kept the shade in his bedroom perpetually drawn, and whenever he exited the house it was out the back door and through the alley. In time, Tim made new friends outside the neighborhood, friends he never invited over for fear of their being influenced by The In-between. He grew protective of these new acquaintances and had no intention of introducing them to the nightmare woods.

During the months and years that followed, Tim would occasionally wonder about the progress being made on the foundation and if his friends had continued the excavation alone or if they had recruited others. His curiosity was never enough to investigate, but still, there was always that longing to know. He did not doubt that The In-between desired his return, so it went without saying that it still had a minor influence over him. The hold over his friends, though, was far worse. School seemed to bring out the worst in them—that is, when they chose to attend—and they never once acknowledged Tim when they passed him in the hall. They had shunned everything and everyone in their life, all but The In-between.

Now, as Tim walked the quiet trail of The In-between, he felt the past closing in, enveloping him with each step. It felt as though no time had passed, that he was still that young kid who had promised himself never to set foot in these woods. He half expected to hear the distant clang of shovels hitting stone, and this thought led him to wonder again if the mullet boys had been real or a figment of his imagination.

Twigs broke behind him, and when he turned he had his answer. Two of the mullet boys wended their way around him as if he was nothing but an obstacle in the woods. He watched as they strode along the path, each holding what at first appeared to be a mass of fur in their hands. It was only when Tim noticed their bald heads that he realized each held not the pelts of recent kills but their mullet-styled wigs. Tim was left dumbfounded at the sight, wondering if the shaving of one's head and the bearing of an accompanying wig was some sort of initiation into this kid gang. What walked ahead of him was a new breed of boy, and Tim was grateful to be standing. They might just as well have clubbed him to death for trespassing in their woods.

One of the mullet boys stopped momentarily. He turned his head and motioned for Tim to follow. There was no threat in the gesture, and while Tim was hesitant, he started forward at a cautious pace, paying close attention to his periphery in case of an ambush. The longer he walked, the calmer he became, experiencing a euphoria he had not felt since those early days of fort-building. He longed to catch up with the boys, these extensions of his lost childhood friends. There was a disturbance at his side, and he watched as another hooligan rushed past. This one was younger than the rest, not yet fully indoctrinated into the group—his mullet still had the appearance of the real thing, not a facsimile.

The group, including the newcomer, disappeared around a bend concealed by deeper foliage. Tim was not worried in the least. He took his time walking the path, admiring the beauty of The In-between as though for the first time. In many ways, this place had always been his home, a place of refuge, a haven fashioned for him alone. His friends had had similar selfish views, but that was fine because there was more than enough for everyone. There always would be.

Tim arrived at the hidden bend in the woods, knowing what lay beyond. In his mind's eye, he saw it as it had been. But when he stepped into the clearing and glimpsed what now tainted the land, he collapsed to his knees. The size and scope of the project was awe-inspiring. Tim cupped his ears and pushed against his skull as if to halt the image that was already burning into memory. The sound of heavy labor poured into his muffled ears, and to him it was the sound of evil.

Tim rose to his feet and moved sluggishly forward, feeling as though his movements were not his own, as though some primal part of himself was reacting to a summons that his conscious mind could not hear. Nearly four feet of the massive structure had been excavated, and its breadth was staggering to behold. As a boy, Tim had only ever glimpsed a small portion of the structure's surface. He stared at the mullet boys—this new generation of slave—who stood sentinel-like along the foundational roof. They were watching him, not with menace but welcome. There were a dozen of them, all shirtless and bald, their wigs tucked beneath their belts.

Tim felt a vice-like pressure on his wrists. To either side of him stood a mullet boy, leading him forcefully forward. Tim did his utmost to break free, but either he had grown exhausted or these lissome juveniles were superhuman. They escorted him to an opening in the foundation wall . . . and at long last Tim saw the extent of the excavation that had begun with his friends and been continued by this most ambitious generation of boys.

A vast staircase descended into the lower depths, its stone rungs disappearing into the pitch darkness twenty feet down. Tim sensed that these stairs dropped infinitely further than that. He took a step back, but that was as far as he got. The strength of his executioners was beyond compare. They dragged him down the first few steps, the tips of his shoes having created tiny ruts along the forest floor, and as darkness tore at his senses, Tim unleashed a scream that echoed into the heart of the monstrum below.

DUPLEX

WE'VE BEEN LIVING in the duplex for nearly a month and have yet to meet our neighbors.

My husband Greg fills their absence with his typical flights of fancy, imagining them as creatures of the night. *It's only a matter of time before they return to roost and suck our carcasses dry.* This, in his best Bela Lugosi imitation. After the move, whenever I complained of lingering aches, Greg would examine my neck for entry wounds, discovering nothing but the usual scattering of moles— a few of which he claimed never to have seen before. He would then angle his incisors toward my neck, lips smacking grotesquely as he traversed my jugular. Invariably, I would push him away, faux screeching like some petrified scream queen. I had never even been mildly attracted to horror films until I met Greg, and I'm still not particularly keen on them, but with him at my side the stuff is at least tolerable. His knowledge of the genre is infectious, his ardent commentary making our evenings memorable for their humor and quirky good fun.

There's no question that the duplex was a dramatic downgrade, but in the wake of near-parallel divorces, such a decline in lifestyle could not be avoided. Our long-standing affair had caught up with us, as I think we always knew it would—loose ends subconsciously laid, breadcrumbs left about for our respective partners to discover and ultimately confront us with. As chaotic as our dissolutions had been, we were overjoyed to be together. The duplex provided a roof over our heads, and in time I knew it could be *revamped*, to use Greg's preferred term, into a comfortable and inviting space. As resources would be tight for the indefinite future, it would take ingenuity, but I felt up to the task.

This weekend we decided it was time to introduce ourselves to our neighbors. We knocked on their door and listened intently for movement, but we were met with silence. The bay window to the left of the door was draped with a sun-faded beach towel, which to my mind spoke of the hoarder's paradise within. Greg hammered on the door a final time, and after another minute or so the deadbolt shifted in its housing and the door creaked opened, merging with an interior darkness that even the sun could not to penetrate. I suddenly felt paralyzed. The gap continued to widen, not unlike some subterranean maw. And then, as if by some weird illusion, a silhouette cut itself from the greater darkness and stepped to the threshold. Greg did not hesitate to make introductions, though his nervousness was evident. I wasn't able to make out any of the details of the man's face. He stood far enough back to conceal everything but his outline. Greg was explaining the specifics of our move, but the man's only reaction was to shift on the balls of his feet like a child too polite to ask for a restroom. When Greg asked for the man's name, his one-sided conversation came to an end. The door swung shut, and the deadbolt jolted back into place. We waited there, as though expecting the occupant to reappear, to reveal his ruse. But the long silence was enough to make Greg curse under his breath and lead me not back to our side of the duplex but to the sidewalk for a much-needed stroll around the block.

This provided the catharsis we needed after such an unfruitful first encounter with our neighbor. The fact that he—or *they*, we still weren't sure—desired no social contact was nothing to worry over. And, of course, this nearly cemented Greg's creature-of-the-night theory and had him contemplating ways we might protect ourselves with garlic necklaces and such.

Back at home, we spent a few minutes with our ears to the duplex's dividing wall before eventually distracting ourselves with a bit of renovation. Nothing major as we hadn't the wherewithal for any elaborate changes. But we made enough noise to expect retaliation from Mr. Dark demanding quiet. I'll admit to a bit of passive-aggressiveness, seeking to encourage the loner to venture further into the spotlight, extract himself from his shadowy enclave. As we worked, however, we received neither a knock on the door nor on the dividing wall. Had the situation been reversed, had Mr. Dark been the one making such ungodly noise, I would have bared tooth and claw and demanded he cease and desist. When we wrapped things up for the day, I came close to pounding on the wall merely to express my dissatisfaction with his non-confrontational stance. On the bright side, his desire for anonymity beat the alternative of the space containing a horde of unruly children even now driving us to hair-pulling madness.

Later that evening, after purchasing a few items on the cheap at the local grocery, we concluded things with a makeshift candlelit dinner that, after a few bottles of two-dollar wine, had us up and dancing and laughing carefree through the place as though it were the ballroom of some newly ordained French chateau. Neither of us considered how much of a disturbance we were making, and our neighbor, who was the farthest thing from our minds, remained as silent as ever. In time, we collapsed onto the sofa and made it through about ten minutes of the movie we had rented from the library earlier that day. We fell asleep in each other's arms.

When we resurfaced, it was still dark out. Initially, I was surprised that we had woken at the same moment, for Greg could usually sleep through most night-time disturbances no matter the decibel level. I began to tell him of the strange dream I had experienced. Midway through, a look of astonishment washed over Greg and he informed me that his dream had unfolded in exactly the same manner. We decided that each had to have been inspired, and subsequently hatched, by our neighborly encounter. Nevertheless, it was uncanny that the context had been duplicated in such a way, as though the scenario was transmitted by a secret source. In the dream, we had woken in the duplex, which initially seemed normal until we realized that every object within was situated opposite to its normal place. We had entered the bathroom, flicked on the light, and were thrust into white blindness. Our eyes adjusted, and the mirror, like a sheet of developing film, slowly revealed our faces. Or, more specifically, our eyes. And while these eyes were our own, the consciousness behind them was not. We knew this intuitively. This, then, was the trigger that severed us from our nightmare.

We tried falling back asleep after moving from the sofa to the bedroom, but our circadian rhythms also seemed to have been reversed. Perhaps the moon would now be our sun, the darkness our light. As we were considering the implications of this new life-style, a disturbance on the other side of the dividing wall refocused our attention. The unearthly cry sounded as grotesquely beautiful as a newborn's entry into the world, but the scariest part was that it seemed to emanate from an adult throat. Greg and I turned to one another, dumbfounded. Neither of us mistook the cry as a plea for help, though it put us on edge, had us wondering if we were imagining the whole thing or if we were still caught in our dream. In the long silence that followed, we were pleased to be reacquainted with a weariness that in time swept us away.

Sleep embraced us until a little past noon the following day, though we hardly felt refreshed. We managed to drag ourselves from bed and into the kitchen, where Greg brewed a pot of coffee while I sat slumped at the table as if in the throes of a debilitating illness. Greg set a cup before me, but the idea of grasping its handle seemed too much of a physical strain. Even the aroma of the morning brew, normally the most pleasurable part of my day, had me wishing I had remained in bed. As much as I was sure the caffeine would clear the fog of that morning, I could not force myself to partake in a single sip. Greg, on the other hand, did so . . . and spit the contents right back into the cup. His look of disgust shifted to consternation. I think we sensed that a further decline in our condition was imminent. The humorous implications, not to mention the rarity, of going through dual illnesses did not escape us. As we assisted each other like a pair of centenarians to the living room—joking about who would be caretaker—we decided, at least for the time being, to let the glowing balm of television be our first line of defense.

Less than an hour into this unorthodox therapy, I felt the first inkling of discomfort in the back of my throat. A deeper illness was making itself known, signaling as though from my core, and I knew that my downward spiral was far from over. Our downward spiral, I should say, because Greg also complained that his throat felt as though it were being squeezed by invisible hands. In time, all communication was dropped and we continued to zone out in front of the television. For now, I was content to let the ceaseless images wash over me. Staring at the walls, or each other, in our present condition would have been hell.

By evening our conditions had worsened, and the medicine I found wedged in the back of the kitchen cabinet was incapable of soothing any of it. Somehow I found the strength to extract a pan from the cupboard to heat a can of chicken noodle soup, though Greg had to help with the pull tab. The broth relieved our throats, but only temporarily. Toward late evening, I was beginning to feel increasingly despondent and helpless. It felt as though the walls were closing in with each breath I took. There came a point when I suggested to Greg that we force ourselves outside to get some fresh air, even though I knew we wouldn't be able to maintain such extended exertion. I had the unshakable feeling that if we did not escape this pesthouse, even for a short while, our illnesses would advance to the point of us resembling some approximation of the living dead. When I turned toward Greg, I found that he was already asleep, his jaw hanging crookedly like one of those aforementioned ghouls. I tucked in as close to him as I could, and closed my eyes.

I woke late in the night, already aware of activity beyond the dividing wall. It was hard to determine exactly what was going on, but the sound of movement was comforting. There was laughter and muffled conversation, all of it laced with domestic bliss. A nail was being hammered into the dividing wall, and in the silent aftermath, I imagined a print being hung and carefully balanced. I was thankful for such activity, for it had the effect of freshwater waves lapping at my irradiated shore, its healing waters drawing me back to sleep with the promise of full recovery on the other side.

The following morning, when I asked Greg how he felt, he only lay there, eyes open and unblinking. Had it not been for the moistness there, I would have feared that he had died during the night. When he spoke, his voice sounded as garbled as mine. He felt worse than he had yesterday and wasn't sure if he could draw himself from bed. We lay there for what seemed an hour, waiting for any inkling of motivation to hit. We decided it was imperative to visit urgent care, have ourselves examined and prescribed with medication powerful enough to combat whatever it was we were suffering. But the idea of rising from bed, making ourselves presentable, and venturing to the car seemed like a high-wire act we were ill-equipped to perform. We did give it our best effort, however, with Greg managing to open the door and take a few initial steps outside. The intensity of the afternoon light, however, proved too unbearable, and he made a quick retreat, rubbing his eyes as though he had become permanently blind.

We eased ourselves on the sofa, with Greg growing angrier by the moment. He wondered if something inside the duplex was making us sick. There had always been a persistent, musty smell, so the possibility of mold could not be discounted. We needed to get in touch with the landlord and demand that our side of the duplex be properly tested—that, or we would start looking for a different place to live.

Greg was still complaining about his eyes, of a haze that he could not blink away. I assured him that the condition was only temporary, that our bodies were more sensitive in their current states of distress. I had, however, begun to notice a similar change in my own eyesight, a reality distortion that made the contours of the duplex seem more prehistoric, in the sense that the space was beginning to feel more cave-like than man-made. Was it possible that our surroundings were deteriorating as well? And what of the world outside? Had it degenerated into a wasteland? As much as I wanted to discuss these delusional thoughts with Greg, I didn't have the energy to speak. I reached for his hand and clasped it as tightly as I could. Had Greg not been at my side, I was sure that the illness would have claimed me long ago.

A series of knocks on the front door startled us. It was likely a solicitor, so neither of us felt a compulsion to rise. But as the knocks became more persistent, it became clear that the individual knew we were inside. Irritated, Greg forced himself up with a painful grunt. He turned and offered his hand, encouraging me to his side. The knocking continued unabated.

We shuffled forward and, after what felt like an hour, reached the front door. The knocks were so ominous that it felt as though reality was on the verge of collapse. It was only when Greg grasped the knob, and began to twist, that the knocking ceased. He opened the door, and we peered into what at first we thought was a full-length mirror. Its reflection held Greg and I, albeit healthier-looking incarnations. It had to have been a practical joke, though who had perpetrated it I could not say. The man, who looked exactly like Greg, spoke in a voice I had grown so accustomed to over the years. He welcomed us to the neighborhood, stating that he and the woman at his side, that is to say me, lived next to us. As their smiles widened, Greg and I dropped to our knees, our paralysis complete. I wondered how long we would be able to retain this prayer-like pose before arriving at the inevitable end that had been growing in us all this time.

Our neighbors did their level best to placate our worry with good humor and grace, their thoughtful words ushering us into our respective new flesh.

IN DEMONTREVILLE

———— ✦ ————

BEYOND THE BORDER of Demontreville, Iowa, Ray's wife Melissa ordered him to stop the car. She was holding her head, and seemed on the verge of hyperventilating. She was prone to migraines, but this was different—it had come out of nowhere.

Ray pulled to the side of the road and glanced fleetingly into the rearview mirror. He was comforted by their proximity to town. Weathered brick storefronts rose along either side of the main drag, the setup resembling some partially faded past-century post-card. Ray doubted Demontreville contained a hospital, but there was bound to be someone who could help.

Ray undid his seatbelt and shifted closer to Melissa, trying to comfort her. She was drenched in sweat and trembling, leaving Ray to wonder if this was the end, if the love of his life would soon be gone, taken down by some freak aneurism.

Then, just as quickly as it had begun, it was over and Melissa breathed a sigh of relief. She turned to Ray, her uncertain smile shifting to strained laughter before she collapsed into his arms. She spent a minute hugging him before she pushed away and exited the vehicle. Ray followed and walked to her side. The sun was intense and sweat was already starting to bead his forehead.

"It's okay...I'm okay," Melissa whispered, clasping Ray's hand and drawing him close. "I don't know what that was, but I'm not sitting in that car for another second." She raised her head to have a look around. "Where are we, anyway?" She squinted into the distance, trying to read the sign at the edge of town.

"Demontreville," Ray said. "Population 54."

Melissa turned away from him and started walking toward town, moving at a brisk pace. She seemed to have fully recovered.

"Hey, wait up," Ray called after her. "It's a bit farther than you think." And it was: for each step they took, the town seemed to recede an equal distance, not unlike a mirage.

Melissa turned briefly, encouraging him on. "There's gotta be a general store or something where we can get a drink. I don't know why we didn't stop in the first place."

Ray knew exactly why they hadn't, and her statement surprised him, for she'd been the one to suggest that they bypass Demontreville. And there'd been good reason: the town wasn't much to look at. Many of the businesses were boarded up, and the few that were open did not look particularly inviting.

They had visited numerous other derelict towns during their weekend excursions—some worth investigating, others not. Nearly a year ago, on their first date, they had discovered a mutual interest in road-tripping. A near obsession, in fact, one that grew by the week. Come Friday, after their respective workday ended, they would unfold the worn state map on the dining table, drinking wine and finger-scanning the many offerings on display. Often, their weekend destination would come about merely by how enticing a place-name sounded. Most times these excursions turned out to be a delightful surprise, though there had been the occasional letdown. The thrill, however, lay in the unknowing, the spontaneity.

Demontreville had not been their destination of choice this weekend, and thank goodness for that. The place looked like a ghost town, at least to Ray. To him, the only enticement of such a town was in capturing its dereliction in a photo or two. With that in mind, he withdrew his phone, angling the screen to capture Melissa striding toward town. This would furnish a bit of comic relief, for she'd certainly get a kick out of the purposefully askew image, especially after he applied a sepia filter. He returned the phone to his pocket and sprinted to Melissa's side, slipping a hand into hers. Judging by her grip, she was back to her old self.

As they approached the first building, Ray stopped in his tracks.

"I forgot the keys," he said, patting the pockets of his jeans.

Melissa turned. "Don't worry about it," she said. "Who here would possibly want that wreck?" She leapt up the steps to the porch of a combination restaurant and hotel. The door behind its screen was open, though the place bore no sign indicating whether or not it was serving customers. The windows were filmed with dust, making it impossible to tell if anyone was inside.

"Appears to be open," Melissa said, approaching the door.

"*Yes, ma'am,*" a voice piped from within, "*that we are.*"

Ray followed Melissa inside, and they were greeted by a thin, wiry man dressed in old-fashioned garb.

"First customers of the day. Please, do make yourselves at home. I am Mr. Paetz." He gave a slight bow. "Where you folks coming from? Up north?"

Ray hesitated. "Up north, yes. From the city," he offered, pointing absurdly skyward.

"Ah, I see . . . Well, it's good of you to have stopped. Demontreville isn't too much visited these days."

Ray wanted to tell the man that in actuality it hadn't been their intent to visit, but he held his tongue.

Melissa spoke for him. "It certainly seems like a charming enough town."

"Well, that's fine of you to say, ma'am, thank you. But the fact of the matter is that our numbers have been dwindling over the years. Used to be vibrant, back when I was a lad. People leave, they pass on. It's nature's way, I suppose."

Melissa moaned, and brought her hands to her head again. "Oh god, Ray, I think it's back," she gasped, leaning into him. He steered her to the nearest table, easing her into a wooden chair. She spread her elbows onto the table's surface, and thrust her head in between.

"Is there anything I can do?" Mr. Paetz asked, hands clasped.

"Just a little space is all," Ray said. "Maybe a glass of water?"

"Of course," the proprietor said, making a quick retreat into the back of the restaurant.

Ray attempted to comfort Melissa, feeling as helpless as he had in the car. She raised her head awkwardly, lips heavy and quivering, eyes wet and bloodshot. "Christ, what's happening to me?"

When Mr. Paetz returned, Ray took the proffered glass and set it on the table. "Drink some, honey. It'll make you feel better."

"Yes, indeed," the proprietor said. "The water here is as pure as it comes. Drawn daily from the spring at the edge of town."

Again Melissa raised her head, as though drawn to the man's voice. She pulled the glass to her lips and gulped the contents.

"Care for another, ma'am?" the proprietor asked.

Melissa licked her lips, searching for a last drop. "Please."

The proprietor nodded. "Anything for you, sir?"

Ray shook his head. "I'm fine, thank you." After Mr. Paetz had gone, Ray turned to Melissa: "Bad as the last one?"

"Not quite, but I think I really need to rest awhile."

The proprietor, having silently reappeared, said: "That can certainly be arranged." He held the refilled glass reverently against his chest. "You're welcome to use one of our upstairs rooms."

Melissa reached for the glass of water, and this time savored it a bit more slowly.

"We can bring a meal up later, if you wish," the proprietor said.

Ray turned toward the man, curious. "We?"

"Yes, sir. The wife and I." He extended an arm toward the stairwell adjacent the far wall. "Show you to your room?"

Ray would much rather have returned to the car, but he grasped Melissa's hand and followed the old man.

The stairs creaked horribly under their collective weight.

AFTER MELISSA FELL ASLEEP, Ray went to the single window overlooking Main Street, eyes flitting from one exterior detail to another. There were times when he thought he detected motion in the corner of his eye, but when he shifted his gaze to the suspected spot, he found nothing. Had it been a Sunday, Ray would have understood this unnerving lack of activity—but, then again, perhaps Saturdays in Demontreville were equally revered.

There was a tap at the door. "Sir?"

Mr. Paetz stood in the doorway, bearing a tray of food. "I thought you and the missus might be hungry. Nothing fancy, mind you. Meatloaf and potatoes. We like to keep things simple here."

Ray became aware of his empty stomach. He hadn't eaten anything substantial since breakfast. "Very thoughtful of you, thanks. I think we'd like to make arrangements to spend the night."

Mr. Paetz smiled. He set the tray on a nearby table. "You are more than welcome to do just that. And you needn't worry about compensation, as I feel somewhat to blame for your wife's upset."

The man's generosity felt suspicious to Ray, and he reached into his pocket for his wallet.

"I meant what I said, sir. Forget about this day's unfortunate events and start tomorrow fresh. Things will be brighter then. And don't forget your meal . . . it's on its way to getting cold."

The proprietor retreated to the stairwell. "Sleep well, sir."

Ray grabbed the tray and returned to the window. He pulled up a chair, resting the tray on his knees and shoveling forkfuls of meatloaf and mashed potatoes into his mouth.

He considered venturing outside for a brisk walk, if only to retrieve the car and park it closer to town. He'd feel better knowing it was nearby, locked and with the keys on the nightstand. But leaving Melissa was out of the question. He needed to be here in case she woke up.

It was beginning to darken outside, and Ray searched the room for a lamp. He found one on the antique dresser across from the bed. It was filled with oil, and a box of matches was set at its side. This was undeniably part of the establishment's charm, Ray thought, catering as it did to city folk desiring an escape from the trappings of the modern world.

Ray approached the bed and lay next to Melissa. She was breathing in that rhythmic, soothing way that had always encouraged his own entry into sleep. In the receding light, he kept his gaze fixed on Melissa's soft features, until darkness swallowed him whole.

WHEN HE WOKE the next morning, Ray felt a persistent pain in his lower back. The light in the room was murky, mostly due to the grime-encased windowpanes. He moved to the edge of the bed, rubbing his eyes, wondering with a start where Melissa had gone. Not yet ready to stand, he groggily called out her name.

Typically, he woke whenever there was the slightest disturbance in their bed, so it was surprising that Melissa had so easily slipped away. Ray went to the mirror on the far wall, stepping close to its warped surface. It was difficult to make out his reflection, but to him he seemed to have aged ten years. He headed for the door.

Downstairs, he expected to find Melissa at breakfast, but the restaurant was as empty as it had been yesterday.

In all likelihood, Melissa was exploring the town. She had always loved striking up conversations with residents and business owners, inquiring about their lives—what made them tick, their small-town philosophies. Ray loved that about her.

Once outside, he checked on his car. It shimmered in the distance like a mirage, winking in and out of existence as heat waves rolled along its surface. He thought of jogging out there to retrieve it, but finding Melissa took precedence. He made his way along the wooden sidewalk, amazed by the vibrancy of the town. Unlike yesterday, none of the businesses he passed were boarded up, and each of them contained at least a dozen patrons. But the strangest thing of all was that everyone was dressed in 19th-century period costume. Ray felt as though he were walking through some historical reenactment.

He about to make his way back to the restaurant when he saw Melissa. She was walking along the opposite sidewalk, and as Ray called her name, she stepped into a building. He ran to the storefront in question and pushed through the door. A bell pinged above him, announcing his presence.

Melissa was behind the front counter, organizing items on its surface. The place appeared to be a general store, and as much as Ray wanted to examine the surroundings, he kept his focus on Melissa. She was dressed in an old-fashioned gingham dress, as though she, too, were part of the reenactment.

Ray went to the counter. "Hon," he said, his tone on the verge of laughter. "I've been looking all over for you. What's going on?"

She looked at him with a smile that chilled Ray to the core. "Anything I can help you find today, sir?"

Ray felt his stomach shift. "This isn't funny, Melissa. Well, okay, it kind of is, but..."

"May I ask where you're from?"

"*Where I'm from?*" Ray said this a bit too loudly. All the patrons in the store stopped their browsing to stare at him. "Come on now, hon, this is ridiculous." He reached across the counter and grabbed her wrist. "Come on, it's time to go. Joke's over."

Melissa pulled free just as another worker stepped from the back room. "What seems to be the trouble, sir?"

Ray fumbled for words. "Mr. Paetz," was all he could summon.

"Yes, I am Ezra Paetz," the man confirmed with cautious pride.

Ray felt weak. What was going on here? He could understand Melissa playing a practical joke, but Mr. Paetz as well?

The old man whispered something, and when Ray heard the words—*Do you know this gentlemen?*—he snapped.

"Melissa, it's time to go!"

Mr. Paetz took a step back with Melissa in tow.

"Sir, I think it would benefit us all if you were to leave."

Ray shook his head in disbelief. "I'm not sure what's going on here," he said, loud enough for everyone to hear. He waited for the denouement of this practical joke to arrive, for everyone to point and laugh at his naiveté and reveal their carefully constructed ruse. But everyone remained silent.

"I'll get the car now, Melissa," he said. "And then we're leaving." He turned and exited the store and began loping down Main Street. In the distance, his car appeared to be disappearing. He sprinted the rest of the way, relieved when his palm made contact with its hot, solid surface.

Ray felt energized once he was behind the wheel. He started the engine and idled for a moment, staring at the road ahead and wondering how far it was to the next town. He dismissed the urge to open the glove box and consult the state atlas. Melissa had always been the navigator. He'd wait for her to join him.

He imagined them at home, snug on the sofa with a bottle of wine, watching an old black and white movie. Maybe they'd take a break from travel for a while.

Ray inched the car around until it pointed in the direction of town. He hit the accelerator, but faltered soon after.

In the distance, Demontreville shimmered in and out of existence like a mirage. And then: empty countryside.

Melissa was still in Demontreville.

Wherever it was.

MARGINALIA

———◆———

JULIA HAS GROWN ACCUSTOMED to hesitating at the threshold of her father's room, knocking at the always-open door and offering her standard *Daddy, I'm here*, even if the end stage of his illness has rendered such pleasantries meaningless. It's a ritual, however, one she refuses to break. And even though her father no longer responds, or registers her presence, it's not difficult for her to dig into memory and resurrect his assured voice. In the early days of his incarceration at the nursing home, his reply had always been a vibrant *Enter, young lady*. That voice, and the sharp mind behind it, had buoyed Julia through her formative years, and she desperately misses it. Eyes closed, clinging to the threshold, she nearly convinces herself that his voice is even now resonating from the shadowed bed along the far wall. But such trickery is short-lived, for when Julia opens her eyes and takes her first step into the room, the illusion fades to the cold reality of a small gray space no more inviting than a prison cell.

Last week, the staff director had informed her that Lane was in his final decline, that only a month remained. If she looked at the situation with a clear and rational mind, she knew that the man who had once been housed within the currently bedridden body had died last month. The day was still clear in her mind. She had been standing near the bed, gazing uncomfortably into Lane's eyes until he piped up, with surprising anger, to proclaim that he had no idea who she was and that she had no right to be there. Julia had calmly attempted to stir up memories she knew must only be hiding, but during the ten minutes she had tried to connect with Lane she had grown so unnerved by his confrontational stance that she had no choice but to leave. She had held back tears while in her father's presence, but in the corridor outside his room, she had collapsed against the cold wall and wept. She had known that such a turning point would eventually arrive—the staff had outlined the stages of the illness and what she could expect from each—but to be in the midst of it for real was too much. In the back of her mind, she had always assumed that a scientific advancement would be announced, or that her father would figure a way to combat the blight that ravaged him. Nevertheless, she had continued her daily visits, thinking that showing up would be enough to halt her father's steady march toward the abyss, that the damage that had already been done would scab over and heal with time. But it was all delusion. The abyss was insatiable, luring bits and pieces into its maw: memory, speech, movement, all of it disappearing. As Lane's sole caregiver, Julia had had nowhere to turn but herself, and as the days and months ticked by, she experienced a mental decline that ran parallel to Lane's. She had even begun wishing for her own memories to be wiped clean, especially those linked to her father.

Now, as Julia advances into the semi-darkened room, she experiences a chill that grows deeper by the step. She can't make out the features of her father's face or form. She can, however, hear his coarse breathing—a faulty bellows that seems to grow in intensity the longer she remains at his side, as though he can detect her presence through some primitive means. Julia walks to the window and opens the blinds. She peers at the busy cityscape, which features a constant flow of traffic and pedestrians. The view has depressed her of late because she can't help but contrast all that burgeoning life with the immobile vessel behind her. Not that Lane had ever complained of this room or its view—his temperament had always been calm and collected. Even the staff had praised the grace and good humor he had shown during the many stages of his illness. With Julia, they had shared stories about residents who had not gone so gently into that good night. It all came down to the personality of the individual.

While Julia regrets having transplanted Lane, there had come a point when she could no longer overcome the challenges of home-care. There were no siblings, and her mother had died a decade before. She couldn't quit her teaching position, and the mishaps at home had become increasingly dangerous, leaving her little choice but to seek help from a facility that could better accommodate her father's failing health. Lane had never complained during the transition, fully accepting his new lot in life. He'd gone through numerous ups and downs during his lifetime, and this was just another challenge to overcome. His stoicism brought Julia to tears on more than one occasion.

In the early days of this new living arrangement, Julia had made sure not only to visit or call regularly, but also to make a point of taking Lane on various outings—field trips, as she liked to call them. She had read numerous stories online about residents who, once freed from the confines of a care facility, begged and pleaded not to be taken back, becoming belligerent during their forced return. But not so with Lane. From the first, he was a delight to be with, like old times, and their outings were memorable from beginning to end—even if it was as simple as patronizing the nearest ice-cream parlor or sitting on a park bench near the edge of a lake and tossing gobs of bread to ducks. Lane had taken her to similar places when she was a child, and even though the roles were now reversed, they were no less impactful. During such outings, it was easy to tell by the look in Lane's eyes and the overt intensity of his furrowed brow, that he was doing his utmost to take everything in. It was heartwarming and heartbreaking, for Julia knew that the details would likely be forgotten by the following morning. Invariably, there would come a point during their outing when a confused expression would wash over Lane and he would politely ask—in a way that made Julia think she was little more than a paid chaperone—to be returned to his room.

Now, as Julia turns from the window, she feels unbalanced, on the border of two extremes: the grating motion of the outside world and the silent deterioration of this inner one. She thinks of the courage her father showed during his transition, and in a flash of inspiration she comes to a decision. She takes a deep breath and crosses the room to Lane's side. *This can't be you, Daddy.* She eases closer, her focus on the reposed countenance that, in the dim light, resembles porcelain. Lane's eyes are closed, and for the past few days he has been in a near-perpetual state of sleep. His normally angular jaw seems even more pronounced, as though the illness has collected like deadweight in his chin. The shadow-darkened pit of his open mouth unnerves Julia. She reaches out to push the jaw back into place, but then changes her mind when she imagines it clicking shut like the wooden mouth of a ventriloquist's dummy. Nevertheless, she keeps her gaze fixed on the false face, studying its parted hair, overlarge ears, and the long eyelashes that used to flutter against her cheeks when she was young.

Julia turns her attention to the paperback on the nightstand. It is a western that she has been reading to him in installments. Only two chapters remain. She touches its tattered surface, wanting to complete the story for Lane, even though she knows he has read the book numerous times. As though sensing her thoughts, Lane begins to gulp for air. Paralyzed, Julia stares into the pit, waiting for the darkness to widen and absorb not only her father but herself as well. She leans closer and places her lips on her father's forehead a final time. She whispers, certain that those overlarge ears are registering every word, *I'll always love you, Dad.*

Julia stands there as if waiting for Lane to respond, to produce some small acknowledgment of her parting words, a raised finger or a flutter from those distinctive eyebrows. But there is nothing. Just that cavernous insuck and expulsion of air. Julia retreats from the bed, steps into the corridor, and marches through the automated front door of the facility. It is only when she is inside the steel womb of her father's Saab that she breaks down and begins to cry.

THE LONG DRIVE brings little solace to Julia, and instead of veering off the interstate to the thoroughfare that would return her to her childhood home—a property she is intent on selling as soon as possible—she continues north along the freeway, assured by a full tank of gas. After a few miles, a green road sign proclaims the mileage to her destination. During the first weekend of each summer, her family had made the pilgrimage to the North Shore, and the thought of doing so again fuels Julia with hope. Her focus must remain on movement, but she can't stop thinking of Lane—his final moments of life, his final breath. By ending her visitation prematurely, has she encouraged the final knell to toll? Did Lane even registered her absence? As though in answer, a familiar voice whispers in her mind, *Enjoy yourself, Jules. I'll be fine.*

Of all her childhood memories, Julia is most fond of the drives up north. Even now, as the interstate lulls her forward, she can recall the tan station wagon with its faux wood-paneled sides, the luggage stacked neatly in the rear compartment. Julia sat in the back seat, books and notepads and Polaroid a her side. Lane, wearing his lucky fishing cap, would occasionally peer over his shoulder. *Beautiful country, isn't it?* he might say, and Julia would agree as she did now. The natural world always seemed to grow richer with each passing mile and it had been impossible to resist its spell. It had taken precedence over her books and journal, all those "city things." The landscape would become increasingly untamed, and when they reached the lake, when its vastness came into view through the thinning trees, its definition had always seemed off to her. It was more ocean than lake. But what thrilled Julia most was when the car shot through one of the many tunnels that had been carved into the rocky bluffs of the North Shore. Without fail, Julia would take a deep breath, trying her best to hold it for the entirety of their passage through the earth, closing her eyes to better concentrate on the effort. Some of the longer tunnels, however, had left her gasping for breath before the car shot back into light. Lane liked to encourage her, particularly in the more challenging caverns, giving a rundown of their progress, proclaiming how close they were to the exit. *I can see the light at the end. Almost there, Jules.*

It takes Julia three hours to reach the port city that is the gateway to the North Shore. It hadn't seemed that long, and it is only as she laboriously makes her way through this industrial metropolis, layered as it is with leviathan overpasses and thick traffic, that the concept of time again gains oppressive weight. It feels as though another three hours pass while she waits in traffic. Even with the windows up and vents closed, she cannot avoid the toxic intrusion of semi exhaust and various other pollutants rising from the corpse of the city. The place is overwhelming and she prays to be done with it. Everything about the city's decline—its crumbling infrastructure and the lethargic denizens who call it home—resurrect in Julia the image of her bedridden father. She has thoughts of turning around, speeding back the way she has come, and returning to Lane's side to share his final moments. But before she can act, there is a break in traffic and she again gains momentum, until at long last nature returns as the predominant force. The road follows the twisting shoreline of the lake, and as Julia glances into her rearview mirror she can no longer see the nightmare city. She gasps for breath, surprised that she has been holding it so long. The richly defined North Shore opens before her, and she again feels at ease with the decision to come. *I wish you could be here, Daddy,* she thinks. *It's so beautiful.* The light seems different to her now that the wild growth along the shoreline has taken over. Traffic loosens up, and before she realizes it she is alone on this newly paved road. She glances toward the passenger seat and smiles—imagines Lane sitting there with his magnetic smile, the one that always made the world seem right.

As beautiful as the passing shoreline is, and as good as it feels to be free of her burdens, Julia cannot shake the idea that she has made a terrible mistake by abandoning her father. The normal course would have been to linger at the nursing home for however long it took for him to gasp his last. Her presence had been the connection, she knows this, has always known it, and even now she imagines her poor father facing the approaching abyss in silence, left only with the parting words she had bequeathed: *I love you, Daddy.* This might have been enough, but maybe it wasn't. Then again, Lane would have probably dismissed her concern and told her that there was nothing left she could do—that the only thing he desired was a goodbye kiss. That was the type of man he had always been, more concerned about the comfort of others than he was of himself. Julia had done all she could, and for that she should feel proud. Had he been coherent he would have pulled her into a strong embrace and whispered the appropriate words of release, and that would have been that. But part of Julia still believes otherwise, knows that Lane is suffering. She can't shake the image of his cavernous mouth, spread wide in a sustained scream.

Julia's attention shifts to the odometer, and she realizes with a shock that the car is nearly out of gas. Such a trivial matter had been the farthest thing from her mind, and she curses herself for not thinking to stop earlier. She glances anxiously from road to dash, wondering how far into the red she can go before the engine sputters out. Each mile affords a false sense of accomplishment, and as she steers around each bend in the road, she feels that the end of her journey is near.

The engine misfires just as a tunnel comes into view. The opening in the bluff seems to scream, and a moment before the car shuttles into darkness, Julia takes a deep breath. The strip-lighting that lines the roof brings a sense of relief, and she knows it will lead her safely to the other side. The tunnel curves gradually, enough to hide the distance to its exit. Julia feels the car hiccup beneath her, and the lighting above follows suit, momentarily cutting out. This happens twice more before the Saab is terminally silenced. Julia directs the car as close to the wall as she can, and as she does so the strip-lighting goes out. The car scrapes the concrete wall, grinding to a halt. Julia remains rigid in her seat, waiting for the lights to resume service. She turns on the car's headlights, relieved as the beams spear darkness. She has held her breath all the while, and when it breaks she begins gasping for air. The end of the tunnel can't be that far, but the prospect of walking through all this darkness terrifies Julia. She stares into the rearview mirror, praying for a set of headlights. Someone will come. They have to.

After half an hour, knowing that she must act, Julia steps from the car and follows the twin beams of light, hoping that when she reaches illumination's end she will be close enough to the tunnel's exit to glimpse its bright opening. But as the headlights begin to fade into rope-like strands of light, she finds herself faced with the prospect of entering complete darkness. She veers closer to the wall, her fingers drifting along its surface. The concrete is cool to the touch—just like her dead father's skin.

In darkness, Julia becomes aware of a sound that renders everything else meaningless. It is a slow and measured inhalation, followed by an exhalation that tears into Julia's soul, leaving her with the impression that no matter how far she continues into the void, toward an exit she knows no longer exists, she will discover nothing but further degradations of terror. There will be no light at the end, only a perpetual susurrus of breath, carrying her deeper into a place of undying night.

THE OPPOSITE TRACK

———— ◆ ————

In Memoriam Stefan Grabinski

WHEN ZALNY AWOKE, he noticed two men sitting on the plush carriage seat opposite his own. Sleep-blind as he was, he could make out little of their features, though they appeared well dressed, like businessmen. He couldn't remember if the compartment had been empty when he'd fallen asleep—and, anyway, hadn't he specifically requested a single room? As with his thoughts, his eyes were reluctant to bring anything into focus. He blinked repeatedly, scrunched his nose, and repositioned himself on the seat. As he did so, he was humored to find that the individuals across the way not only replicated his movement but also coalesced, merging with one another until a single figure remained—a figure who sat bolt upright and glared with a ferocity that chilled Zalny to the core.

There was something oddly familiar about this man, though further speculation was interrupted when Zalny focused on the

97

interloper's eyes, the pupils of which seemed magnetized to their partner. Did he, too, glimpse separate entities, or was he merely mocking Zalny? He studied the man's features more closely, startled by the aquiline nose, high forehead, jutting chin, and attached earlobes. He recognized it all. How many times had he criticized such features in his own bathroom mirror? The only details that differed between himself and this man was the carefully clipped hair, the businesslike attire, and that godforsaken strabismus—which at this stage seemed permanent. Zalny had never been one for hygiene, letting his hair grow past his shoulders, allowing his clothes to disintegrate without repair. Writing was the only activity he had ever cared to keep in check, to perfect in his own way—though even that strange fabric seemed in need of continual tailoring.

The *Noctua* Express rattled and clanked beneath his feet, breaking Zalny's reverie and returning his focus to the mute lookalike. The cross-eyed buffoon's gaze was so intense that Zalny felt pinned, like some rare insect, to the seat cushion. Surely, it was mere coincidence that they shared so many features. The man swayed to accommodate the train's motion, making Zalny think of a department store mannequin on the verge of toppling. He scooted substantially to his right, relieved when his double did not replicate the movement. His attention was pulled toward the drawn curtain, and he lifted a corner of its silken fabric to peer at the shuttling landscape beyond.

It was still dark out, but the moon was full, silhouetting various tracts of land. It was an inspiring sight, leaving Zalny regretful of having no materials with which to write. When he connected with his sister in Prague, and eventually settled into her spacious flat, he promised to record this experience and more. For now, he loaded each detail into the revolver of his mind, pushing aside the dark memories that vied to resurface. So much had been lost as of late … but no, best not veer onto that hopeless track. Zalny continued his study of the crepuscular world, riding the rails of Imagination, shunning the vicissitudes of existence.

Try as he might, Zalny could not elude the sensation of being stared at. In the pane of glass, he glimpsed his companion's reflection and, in a fit of anger, he shot the man a brutal glare, certain that his expression was more potent than any spoken sentiment. The insensitive soul had refused to mind his own business—well, so be it! Perhaps Zalny could extract something useful from the blockhead's life story, use pieces of it in some future fiction. Maybe the strabismus?

"Heading to Prague, are you?" Zalny inquired, astonished and irritated to discover that the man's lips had moved in sync with his own. This "other" was mocking him!

On the verge of berating the man, Zalny hesitated. Beneath the man's perfectly manicured mustache—whose tips reminded Zalny of opposing swords—a smile spread, and in a scene that brought to mind some crazed puppet theater, the eyes *popped* back into place and the strabismus was no more. The resemblance between Zalny and this strange traveler became even more pronounced.

The man whispered, though it was too faint to make out.

"Sorry, didn't catch that," Zalny said, a note of perturbation in his voice. He waited for the man's lips to mimic his own, but the sinister smile held.

The man leaned forward like a wind-up toy, as though wishing to impart some inner secret. His movement was imprecise, reminding Zalny of a wooden art doll being positioned by invisible hands. He worked his jaw in a circular fashion, and all the while the bones clicked.

"Good evening," he said, his tone precise. "And . . . *goodbye*."

Zalny felt his eyes drawing crossways into themselves, and he watched in helpless fascination as the man again became a blurred double of himself—

—and he was falling through space, pouring through the floor of the *Noctua* like a ghost, the components of his flesh as unfocused as his vision.

A SCREECHING OWL jolted Zalny back to consciousness.

Above him, the canopy of stars spread far and wide. It was awe-inspiring, though he had to wonder where the roof of his garret had gone. Or was this merely a new chapter in the dream he had experienced? He repositioned himself on the uncomfortable bed and felt bits of gravel bite into his palms.

Good evening and . . . goodbye. The phrase echoed in Zalny's mind, and a sense of desperation hit when he realized that the dream, if dream it was, had yet to surrender its hold.

The moon afforded some definition to the landscape, highlighting the tracks of steel that extended like lines of quicksilver into the darkness. The *Noctua* had ejected him, left him here. But why? As if in answer, Zalny heard the far off wail of a train, and in his mind's eye he watched as it scuttled further into nothingness.

He lifted himself upright but a dizzy spell threatened to toss him back to the tracks. When the sensation passed, he cupped his hands to his mouth and almost called out, before realizing the futility of the act. The train was long gone, and his dapper double had gone with it. Zalny kicked frustratedly at the gravel beneath his toe, and screamed at length, thinking *Blasted motion demon!*

The owl responded in kind, still hidden away on some perch of darkness. As Zalny attempted to determine its location, he felt his forearms ripple with chills. He took a deep breath and started walking along the tracks, keeping up a continual monologue of his movements, sharing a play-by-play to no one but himself.

He thought again of his expulsion from the *Noctua*. In a way, it seemed only logical, given his longstanding view that the universe was out to get him. It had decreed him uselessness and was now routing him out. This conceit was nothing new to Zalny. He'd used similar scenarios in his fiction, scenarios that oftentimes took on a life of their own. The apartment fire was a perfect example, but this recent "debarkation" from *Noctua* had proven nearly as demeaning. When he made it to Prague and got situated in the room his sister had so graciously offered, he'd turn this experience into his greatest literary achievement. All he need do now was survive. The thought of curling over a desk with pen and paper gave impetus to his finding a way out. And if all this was a dream—how could it not be?—he'd still work it into his fiction. Dreams and reality were sometimes so indistinguishable, and each inspired his pen in equal measure.

Then again this might be the end of the line. In a way, the stifling darkness reminded him of his burning garret, of the demon flames that had not only gutted his living quarters but the contents of his life's work. Everything had happened so fast. He hadn't even been able to salvage his favorite pen. When he had watched the conflagration from the safety of the cobbled street below, he had felt numb and confused. Every time he chanced look at those gathered about, he noticed their accusatory glares, as though he alone had been the author of the flames.

And maybe, in some subconscious way, he had been. Perhaps his failures had gotten the upper hand, forced him awake late that night in a somnolent stupor, compelled him to light the match that birthed such a colossus. His co-tenants had never really cared for him, sharing little else but sneers and whispered declamations when he chanced pass them on the stairs. In a way, Zalny supposed they were right. He had squandered nearly all of his inheritance, and had focused on little else but his pens and paper. But what good was the act of writing if none but himself read his words? Then again, maybe history would be kinder. Perhaps one day his works would be adored, and he, in turn, become Immortal.

Fashioning *fantastique* was his sole joy in life—to write, to shift reality like some minor god, to will something into existence and weave its strands into a cozy, unsuspecting reality. So, yes, maybe he had willed the fire. But even if his words had turned to ash, it was all still firmly embedded deep within him. In time, he would rise like a phoenix from the ruin, stronger and more resilient than ever. His expulsion from the train, as Zalny-inspired as it was, would neither hinder nor harm his creative impulse. He would use it as a springboard to further creation.

As if to confirm or deny such sentiment, the owl again screeched from its hidden enclave. The sound terrified Zalny, and in his mind he conjured a monstrosity that rivaled his known idea of *Strigidae*, something larger and more grotesque, something as hungry and desirous of destruction as any of his literary predators had ever been, something that sought to eviscerate all work he dared create.

He again recalled the phrase that had prefaced his ejection from the train—*Good evening and . . . goodbye*—and wondered if it held some incantatory power to shift reality. With that in mind, he said the words aloud, imagining as he did so a train speeding down the tracks, already on the verge of opening its maw to swallow and reinstall him onto the plush seat and properly escort him to Prague. He thought of the individual who had been the author of this expulsion, wondering if he had been a figment of his imagination or a representation of the man he might have become had he chosen another path, another track.

Zalny again pondered the idea of dreams and how he might wake from this one. Maybe he could throw himself in front of the next oncoming train, force his consciousness into the land of the living with a bright jolt to the brainpan.

In the distance, as if in response to this idea, a pinpoint of light became visible. Zalny followed its movement—a swaying from side to side, producing a hypnotic effect—and the longer he did, the more convinced he became that it was the lamp of a track-walker. He quickened his pace, hopeful that the walker might provide an answer to the question of his whereabouts.

Zalny strode toward the light, but even as he quickened his pace, it seemed that he was making little progress. He cupped his hands and called as loudly as he could, but there was never any indication that the trackwalker had heard his pleas.

Eventually, Zalny arrived at a section of track that split off from the main and continued along a gradual curve toward the hills to his left. While it was difficult to tell which direction the track-walker had gone, Zalny took a chance and struck out on the opposite track, figuring he could always retrace his route. As he did so, he noticed the light slowly shifting in his direction.

He followed the tracks and in time detected the outlines of a figure bearing a lantern. It was impossible to make out a face, but this did not prevent Zalny from trying to summon the trackwalker, pleading for him to wait, that a lost traveler was in need of assistance. Shortly thereafter, the light winked out.

Zalny fell into a clumsy sprint, stopping only when he arrived at the base of the hill, guided now by a fainter light emanating from the rim of a tunnel entrance. He called repeatedly into the maw before proceeding inside, surprised to discover that it was not a tunnel, but a cave. The tracks disappeared into the back wall, and standing between the rails was the trackwalker. It was difficult to make out the man's face, for he had set the lantern on the ground between his feet. He was either mute or waiting for Zalny to take the initiative.

The first utterance, however, was of the ground shifting forcefully beneath Zalny's feet. He sensed a cave-in and turned the way he had come, watching in horror as the rim of the cave crumbled and began to collapse, though not in the usual sense. It seemed as though an enormous mouth, or beak, was closing, extinguishing the stars and the world beyond. In little time, the upper and lower portions of the cave clicked together and the notion of further collapse faded for good.

Zalny slowly eased himself about, ready to commiserate with the trackwalker. But in the flickering glow of the lamp, he witnessed something that annihilated any thought of companionship. The man, whose owlish features were prominently on display, glared at him, a look of diabolical hunger radiating from his overlarge eyes. Zalny could do little else but scream at the implications of such a grotesquerie.

As the lamp guttered out of existence, Zalny heard the first of a series of mind-numbing shrieks, the sound filling the enclosed chamber and tearing into his soul like a multitude of owls alighting on their prey. He could do little else but raise his arms and embrace his most elaborate rejection yet.

COLD BLACK WIND

———— ✦ ————

I DIDN'T WANT to come. Places like this, as embarrassing as it is to admit, have always unnerved me. My father, rest his soul, took me to one at far too impressionable an age, and I've never gotten over the experience. But it was either coming here this evening or picking up the pieces after another hour-long meltdown. Once Jonas latches onto an idea, I've learned that it's best to acquiesce. And the sooner, the better. It's been an exhausting and anxiety-filled few years, but I'm learning—as our ASD therapist would say—to choose my battles. Easier said than done, but I'm getting there. I really am. Or maybe I'm not.

So here we are, Jonas and I, standing before the entrance to Zephyr's first annual winter maze. Jonas is calm, which is such a rarity these days. He gazes with silent awe at the ten-foot high ice-block walls (three times his stature), and I wonder if he's reconsidering his decision to come. If this outing does not meet his expectations, we're in for another public horrorshow, and I'm not sure I'll be able to handle it this time. I can't help but visualize the tantrum to come, and I'm already bracing for such an eventuality.

Jonas punches out with both arms and raises them over his head, a gesture of victory. *This is freaking awesome!* he exclaims, emphasizing each word. His arms return to his side, and I again clasp his hand, giving it a gentle squeeze. I close my eyes and breath a sigh of relief. When I open them again, I feel somewhat reborn. I foresee a pleasant evening, one of those rarities that I can look back on and take strength from. *It is wonderful, isn't it?* I say, though I'm sure Jonas hasn't heard, he's so mesmerized by the icy wonder before him.

A flood of projected light (meant to replicate the aurora borealis) swirls ethereally over the surface of the maze, and hidden speakers pump out a continuous stream of holiday cheer. As much as I dislike this type of music, I find myself strangely soothed. I haven't felt this relaxed in years, even with my aforementioned phobia. Jonas will be nine next month, and his diagnosis at six feels like a lifetime ago. But as we stand here in this winter light, I feel content, as though I've regained something. I wonder, as I have on so many other occasions, how long it will last. It never does, but it's easy to trick myself into thinking it will.

I squeeze Jonas's hand, feel a tug at my arm . . .

And watch as my wild boy bolts headlong into the maze.

I remain where I am, Jonas's mitten drooping like a woolen tongue in my hand, and try to steel myself against a resurgence of the old anxieties. I feel the stares of nearby patrons waiting to enter the maze, each withholding the declaration that has come to define my life: *Your child is out of control. Do something.* Why had I thought that this particular outing would be any different from the previous? A cold numbing sensation creeps from my feet to my neck, and time seems to stand still. Part of me turns and walks away, while the other ventures forward—and the pull from each keeps me right where I am. Stuck in a purgatory of indecision.

I steel myself with reserves I did not know that I had, and, stuffing the mitten into my coat pocket, step through the entrance. I take a deep breath, assuring myself that Jonas will be fine, that I will be fine. Knowing him, he has likely already arrived at the center of the maze. From the website map that I studied the previous evening, the architecture of this place is none too elaborate. Simplicity was built into it, unlike that godforsaken corn maze my father subjected me to. A few missed turns here and there, but everyone—particularly the young, the elderly, and the anxiety-prone—eventually reaches its center.

As I make my way through the initial corridors, I am reminded, strangely enough, of the day that Jonas was born. It had topped one-hundred degrees that day, which for the end of March was unheard of in our northern clime. A fluke event. And to my mind Jonas was the core of that singular weather system. Forever marked by heat, he hasn't stopped moving since. I half expect to discover a path of melted snow carved out by his fiery footfalls.

I turn a corner, then another, feeling a growing chill in the air.

It seeps into my bones, like the fear I felt as a child. Snow begins to fall, lightly at first, and I stop to avert my face to the night sky, feeling enlivened as the flakes land and then quickly melt on my skin. It's a wonderful sensation, and I can't help but smile. Not much has made me smile these last few years.

I continue forward, inverting the collar of my coat. The snowfall increases, and with it a brisk wind pushing through the corridors. The sound of it collects in my ears, a banshee-like wail that heightens my anxiety. I call out to Jonas, and then again in a louder voice. In the silence that follows, I realize that the holiday music has ceased. The steady wind is all that remains, and it feels like a harbinger of worse weather to come. I wonder if I should continue on, or try to retrace my route to the entrance. I plead for Jonas to answer, and in the distance I think I hear a response. I wonder if the wind is playing tricks, encouraging me toward an oblivion that waits at its source. I move through a few more corridors, nearly blinded now by the snow.

Mom, I think I hear, followed by an even fainter *Help, Mom*. I cannot shake the vision of Jonas huddled in a ball in the corner of some dead-end corridor, paralyzed by this surreal downpour of snow. I tell him to keep talking, that I need to hear his voice in order to find him, that I will be there soon.

I slip into another corridor, where a pair of teenage girls are rushing in the opposite direction. I step before them, grabbing one by the coat and asking if she's seen a boy matching Jonas's description. The other teen, the one I am not holding, pushes me to the side, forceful enough to send me plummeting to the ground. As they pass, they utter something that sounds like *You're out of control. Do something.* When I recover my footing, the pain in my hip makes me wince. Everything seems darker now, the light from the faux aurora borealis nowhere to be found.

I need to find Jonas. I need to get out of this maze. It was a mistake to come.

I don't know how many degrees the weather has dropped, but I can feel it deep in my bones. The wind blasting through these corridors feels as thick as a tidal flow, and I can't stop shivering. When I try to call out to Jonas, I find that my jaw barely moves, opening just enough for me to gag on cold air.

In the next corridor, I glimpse a figure laying prone against a dead-end wall. I stop in my tracks, fearing the worst. As I approach, the wind tears at my coat as though attempting to strip me bare. I kneel next to the figure, and my first thought is that it is Jonas's father, gone these past few years to parts unknown. I stare at the black pit of his mouth—spread wide in a long since dissipated scream—and wait for an exhalation that will never come. I take off my glove and check for a pulse at his neck, and the warmth from my fingers seeps through the thin layer of ice that envelopes him like a cocoon. *You were never good for us*, I want to say, but with my locked jaw and dead tongue, the words stay trapped in my mind.

I turn from the frozen impossibility, wondering how long it will be before I succumb to the elements and grow my own fatal skin of ice. I stand against the wall, once again aware of the cold that has seeped into my bones. My legs feel brittle, like icicles that could snap under the slightest pressure. I cover my mouth with my mitten and blow into it until the heat enlivens my musculature. The warmth feels like adrenaline, and once I have reanimated my flesh, I take a final deep breath, remove the mitten from my mouth, and scream Jonas's name at the top of my lungs. I bow my head, close my eyes, and listen.

When there is no response, I continue forward, noticing how very dark it has become. I don't even reach the entrance to the adjoining corridor before the absence of light stops me in my tracks. I reach out to the wall at my side and lean against it. The darkness is so all-consuming, and the more I stare into it, the more I feel as though it is entering through my eyes in an attempt to fill me whole. I could just as well be in an unlit cave deep beneath the surface of the earth.

Nevertheless, I press on, using my mittened hand to follow the wall that leads to the adjoining corridor. I recall the simplicity of the maze-map, but when I think about how much ground I have covered, it strikes me that its online representation is false. This place feels endless, and I wonder if I will ever reach its center, or if my trial will end in some ubiquitous dead-end—one that has waited for me all this time.

I am on the verge of sliding down the wall, succumbing to the horrors of this night, when I detect a gradual lightening in the darkness. I look up and find the moon, slowly shedding its garment of cloud. Its spotlight reveals the wide open space marking the end-point of the maze. A bench carved from a huge block of ice resides at its center, and its intricacy of design is nothing less than surreal. A pole is stuck in its center, at the top of which flaps the Zephyr town flag.

YOU MADE IT! is printed prominently beneath the town seal.

The words are like an insult, and I can't help but take them personally.

I reflect on my failures in life, particularly as the parent of a neurodivergent child. So many mistakes, and each one a block of ice entombing my life.

I scan the area, growing more despondent by the bleak emptiness. I had hoped to find other patrons collected here, but the ice bench is my only companion. I walk to it.

My first thought is to sit, but I know that doing so will be my end. That the cold black wind will infect and dissuaded me from my search. That it will make me forget about Jonas.

And I can't do that. I have so much to make up for. So much yet to give.

Maybe he made it out. Maybe even now he's in the care of some kind stranger who has bought him a cup of hot cocoa while he awaits the return of his lost mother.

And, oh, how very lost I am, I think, before yanking the insulting flag from its hold and tossing it to the ground.

I begin to retrace my route, wishing that I had thought to leave course-markers of some sort. Even my footprints have been lost to the blanket of newly fallen snow.

The only thing that keeps me going is reuniting with Jonas. My flawless, wonderful boy. Never again will I wish that my life had turned out any differently than it has. I have been privileged—why had I not realized this before?—to be in the presence of such a unique child. The idea of our reunion injects heat into my core, and my skin of ice begins to melt.

I will myself forward, moving through the maze at a steady and confident pace. I feel that Jonas is close, my intuition hammering like a second heart. He is so close, I am sure of it. His restless mind is like a beacon, and I feel its palpitation with each step. I long to pull him into my arms and squeeze him tight, even if I know such affection and sensitivity will drive him mad. It always has. *Throw a fit, Jonas,* I think, *and I will join in your wild dance.*

The light from the moon has returned in full, and even the weather seems to have shifted, lost a bit of its harshness. I repeatedly call Jonas's name, my jaw and vocal cords no longer imprisoned by the elements. It feels good to do so, and I don't mind the repetitiveness of it because it reminds me of Jonas, of his hyper-adamant nature, his inability to back down once obsession sets in. We are more alike than I ever knew, and this revelation warms my heart. I am flooded with memory. Events that at the time drove me mad, now seem like the most heartwarming of remembrances.

The next corridor I enter seems longer than any of the others. There are no adjoining passages cut into either wall, and when I pause to look over my shoulder, I am shocked to discover that the length I have walked spools out into an even deeper darkness. Though I know I'm not far from the opening I had walked through, it seems to have been sealed over.

I continue ahead, noticing a winterly light in the distance.

Encouraged, I quicken my pace, imagining the glow to be the entry—and thus exit—to the maze. I sense that Jonas and I will soon be reunited, that the first words out of his mouth will be, *What took you so freaking long?* And then, in true Jonas-fashion, he will plant a swift kick to my shin, as he has so often done in the past when things haven't gone to his liking.

If that's all he has to give, I'll take it. I'll revel in the pain.

I continue at a steady pace through the corridor, but the light remains as distant and undefined as ever. I stop in my tracks, suddenly full of worry. What if this is the light at the end, the one that near-death survivors claim to have seen? The dark corridor, the phantom light, it all seems too right not to be real. Is this why I no longer feel the deep chill in my bones? Part of me wants to run in the opposite direction, but the darkness at my back strikes me as a worse fate.

A gust of wind pushes past me, and in it I hear—or imagine I hear—Jonas's voice. It sounds distant and cold. I press on, toward the light, toward my dark angel.

Eventually, the area of exposure becomes more defined. It is not, as I had first assumed, an exit, but a sourceless spotlight illuminating something encased in the ice. Something that at first looks like a hibernating bear cub. But it's what the ice has not encompassed—a child's hand jutting limply from its surface—that changes everything.

I kneel before the hand, and without thought remove my gloves and clasp the appendage between my own. I am surprised by its heat. It is as warm as that day nearly nine years previous, that day when something so very precious came into my life.

I bow my head and rest it on top of our hands. A flood of memories hits me so hard that I again wonder if this is the end, if the memories represent the rerunning of my life before the transition to something new.

If I could go out right now, feeling as I do, I would. The heat from Jonas's hand is so comforting. It radiates through my body, caressing my limbs and heart in a feeling I can't describe other than the comfort it brings.

I lift my head, tears coursing down my cheeks, and stare into the wall of ice.

The light has not changed, but there seems to be more definition to the trapped figure. Jonas's eyes stare at mine, and even though I know they are frozen, I sense a vibrancy of life trapped within. I keep my vision fixed on them, and in my periphery I can tell that something is happening. The warmth that has been transferred to me is recycling back into Jonas, making his features shine all the clearer. There is movement in his face, as though the ice—once as solid as concrete—has loosened its hold under the warmth of such an inner sun.

Our eyes remain locked, but I can detect Jonas's growing smirk. (He never smiles, always smirks.) I mouth the words—*I love you.*

I'll always be here for you. Always—and feel a surge of warmth, like a heartbeat, pass through us. It's not long before this other heart rhythm matches our own, and as it cycles it erodes more of my son's prison. It's only a matter of time before the ice releases its hold.

And when it does, Jonas and I will walk hand in hand through the remainder of this life's maze, as cold and black as it sometimes can be.

AN ILLUSION OF SUBSTANCE

---◆---

As we left Cinéma Les Nemours, I could still sense Anne-Marie's dismay as to my having cut short our inaugural evening stroll through Annecy to take in a French thriller called *La Gorgone*. The irony was that I missed the majority of the film, the old theater's plush seating accommodating my jet lag all too well. I was still groggy as we re-emerged into a now night-eclipsed Annecy, lit up and busier than ever. A crowd of onlookers had filled the main square, their attention rapt on what appeared to be a public statue. They surrounded it, as though to prevent its escape, and for the life of me I couldn't understand the intrigue. I looked at Anne-Marie and could tell by her expression that she knew perfectly well what was going on. She took me by the arm, leading me closer, ignoring my inquiries. As I said, the crowd was spellbound, especially the few children who were out at this late hour. From what I could tell, it was nothing more than the patinated figure of a man who, judging by his clothes and hat, might have been some important individual from Annecy's past, even though I saw no plaque distinguishing him as such. What struck me as strange was that I did not remember seeing the exhibit when we had first passed through the square. My initial thought was that it was a dedication ceremony of sorts, that the monument had been heaved into place as I slept through *La Gorgone*. Anne-Marie and I stepped as close as the crowd would allow, and it was only when the figure's head shifted downward, its right hand angling toward a bowl of coins, that I fully understood what was happening. The crowd, acting as a single entity, produced the expected laudatory cry of awe, thereafter dropping coins into the bowl. I sensed Anne-Marie staring at me, and could tell that she had been doing so for the entirety of the act. As we turned from the scene and began making our way toward the hotel, she explained in greater detail the oddity I had witnessed, stating the importance of the living statue, that it was a serious and time-honored vocation in Europe and beyond, with artists going to great lengths to cast themselves in long-term immobile roles, not only in the paints they selected to cover their bodies but in the manner in which they developed their muscles and breathing to approximate stillness, to give an illusion of substance. I grew more and more fascinated by the topic, and later, as we lay in bed watching French television, I could not shake my admiration for such a profession. When I shifted closer to Anne-Marie, with the hope of attending to her own statuesque beauty, I found that she had already fallen asleep. I returned to my side of the bed, flipping through channels for nearly an hour before turning off the set. At first, the darkness seemed as impenetrable as stone, and no matter how hard I tried I could not divert my thoughts from the idea of a living statue. At some point, having grown irritated by the persistent ghostly presence, I felt that I had no choice but to rise from bed and wander about the inordinately quiet room before heading spontaneously out the front door and into town. Even though I could feel the cool evening air on my skin, I knew that I had to be dreaming, because it truly felt as though I were floating over the cobbled lanes, a skeletal kite being drawn by hidden string into the heart of Annecy, into the now uncrowded space of the living statue. He, or *it*, stared at me for the longest time, sizing me up without once moving its eyes, the intensity of its focus increasing with each beat of my heart. I remained as still as stone, waiting for movement, cowering like a child beneath a father's unapproving gaze. Then the eyes clamped shut, their black lids seeming to expand like twin boils of ink intent on nothing more than the complete obliteration of all my senses.

WHEN I REGAINED consciousness it was to an overwhelming brightness followed by the startled expressions of a group of onlookers, young and old, encircling me. I tried to move, but the only limb that felt mobile at this stage was my left arm. It was pointing at the empty bowl on the ground. The audience dispersed, unimpressed, and the bowl remained coinless. I tried to close my eyes, though found this an impossible task. I grew increasingly aware of time, particularly its slow passage, and desperately wished to crack from this shell and enjoy the freedom that had once been mine. More than anything, I longed for Anne-Marie, desired to glimpse her gentle eyes, sure that her presence would awaken me from this nightmare. As it happened, I didn't have to wait long. She stepped into my field of vision, close enough to peer into my eyes. I tried to speak, and the longing, the *need*, must have been evident in my blank expression, for I could detect a look of quiet horror in her features, a flash of terrible understanding. Or was it relief? I attempted unsuccessfully to shift my arms, to embrace her, to comfort what I assumed was a growing trepidation. But all her worry disappeared with the arrival of a man who stepped to her side, his arm wrapped snugly about her waist. Such intimate contact made her smile, and as the interloper turned to have a better look at me, I realized the full horror of the matter, for I had glimpsed such a countenance thousands of times in any number of mirrors. The sheer terror of being unable to close my eyes was impossible to bear, and the scream that so desperately sought release was encased unutterably in the stony musculature of my new skin.

IN THE DUST

———— ◆ ————

INA WAS THE FIRST to glimpse the approaching duster. She turned to her father, her expression direct as any word of warning. Henry confirmed the sighting for himself, sprang to his feet, and started gathering their picnic things. He calmly encouraging everyone to the car. Ina's mother, Caroline, lamented the fact that she had not closed windows prior to their venturing out on this clearest of blue sky days. The storm continued its static approach, the once canvas-clear horizon now filling with the nocturnal art of some dark god whose sole motif was anti-creation. The billowing nightscape was a sight Ina had grown sadly accustomed to. It had become as common as the sky and the earth and everything in between.

Caroline clasped Imogene tightly to her chest, a blanket wrapped about the infant as if in preparation for the piercing winds to come. She ran to the coupe, leaving Ina to retrieve the remaining items with her father. While a sliver of Henry's happy-go-lucky self had returned during their outing today, the blunt stoicism that had marked him like a brand for the past two years resurfaced: *"Hurry up now, we might still beat the devil home . . . "* But Ina knew the truth, knew that they were too far out to make it even halfway to the farm. Nevertheless, she nodded, hopeful that she was wrong, that the storm would shift, head south or dissipate before it reached them.

Ina grabbed the picnic blanket and bundled it in her arms. In the front seat of the coupe, Caroline was staring directly at the duster, her lips shifting in silent prayer. Then, like a lit fuse, she raised her right fist and smacked it on the dash, following this with a desperate, low moan. Ina wished her mother would not so easily give in to despair, wished she still had the fortitude to stand strong against these dust-laden leviathans of their new world. No one in the family had been the same since Jacob's disappearance, this was true. The loss affected each in different ways, though with Caroline it was more outwardly visible.

Ina reluctantly followed her father to the car, wishing more than anything that they didn't have to leave this beautiful spot behind. The change in weather could strike so rapidly these days, and its unpredictability unnerved and enraged her. The storms were unlike anything anyone had ever experienced, composed of dusty topsoil gathered from the drylands of distant counties, thick enough in its makeup to dim the light of the noon sun for hours or days on end, turning a beautiful afternoon into a nocturnal hell. That was a phrase her father often used to describe these worst bad times, and Ina wholeheartedly agreed.

After she pitched the remaining items in the back seat of the Ford, she climbed in and shut the door as hard as she could. The dust would find a way in, of that she had no doubt, but the rageful act left her feeling enervated, ready to face the storm for all it was worth. She watched her father make his way around to the driver's side, hesitating near the hood as though offering a final challenge to the duster—that, or willing it to fizzle out before his eyes. Soon enough, he was behind the wheel, sweat pouring from his forehead, encouraging the temperamental coupe forward. The razor-sharp wind was already tearing at the vehicle's hull—though it hardly mattered, for the coupe had weathered many a storm and had the scars to prove it.

Ina kept silent in the back seat, waiting for her father to speak. What did she expect him to say? They had gone through this so many times, and words never alleviated the anxiety of an approaching duster, nor did they ease the inborn knowledge of what a storm like this could do to anyone caught out in it. The Ford was gaining speed now, her father's hands clenched tightly on the wheel, his body rigid and angled forward as if willing Nature to part this sea of dust, if only for the time it took to arrive home safe and sound. Ina thought she could hear a prayer being uttered from her father's lips, but the wind was so strong now it was impossible to make out the words.

Caroline shifted in her seat. "Ina, would you . . . " But the remainder of the thought was forgotten, swept away as if by a tendril of wind. It wasn't difficult for Ina to fill in the gap, however. She reached into the picnic basket at her side and withdrew three cloth napkins, handing two to her mother and keeping the third for herself. She balled it in her hand and made ready to cover her nose and mouth. The coupe provided one layer again the onslaught of dust, the cloth another. Neither was ever enough.

Ina recalled the fate of the Whitman family, caught as they had been in a similar storm last year, none surviving to tell the tale. Sheriff Henderson had discovered their Dodge half-buried in a drift at the side of the road, their front window shattered and each member of the family riddled with briars from the thistles that had exploded into the interior like buckshot. Incidents such as this were regularly reported in the county newspaper, but the Whitman story had chilled Ina the most, the horrific details having carved a memory as deep as those killing briars. She wondered if her family faced a similar fate. The Whitman's terror was now hers to hold.

Imogene was crying, her screeching intonations muffled due to her proximity to Caroline. Now that the Ford was moving at a quicker pace, Ina could hear the scrape of the drag-wire. Her father had affixed it months ago, and it not only grounded the vehicle but prevented stalling. A static charge had already started fizzling her hair, creating a tickling sensation that was the storm's single delight. The sky was darkening rapidly now, and the winds rocked the Ford like a flimsy vessel on rough seas.

They were still miles from home, and Ina wondered if they would ever see it again. She tried picturing the farmstead in her mind, but it wasn't clear. No matter how hard she tried, she could only imagine the dust and dunes of a landscape turned to further wasteland. She shifted her focus instead to her brother Jacob, to the inevitability that she would soon be joining him. What could possibly exist on the other side of this dust-coated Reaper?

Full dark arrived quick and hard, forcing Henry to bring the Ford to a halt. As he cut the ignition, darkness as dense as ink infiltrated the coupe. The rocking continued, giving the impression that they were still moving swiftly down the road. The scouring wind muffled Imogene's cries, as well as Caroline's pleas to a higher power. Ina could not make out the outlines of her parents or the seat in front of her, even though it was no more than a hand's-length away. It was as if everything had disappeared, as if she alone existed in this murky limbo. She was thankful, then, when her father's voice pierced the veil.

"It's gonna be okay . . . it'll soon pass."

Ina held onto the pronouncement as though it were a talisman. She kept the rag at her mouth, not daring to let any portion of it part from her skin. Dust was still rapidly accumulating inside the coupe, its density like a tightening, gritty caul. Ina hoped that her father was right, that the darkness would soon lift—but she also knew that these storms were anything but predictable. They could last minutes or days.

She heard her mother's voice, a storm of its own that contained hardly a recognizable word. Its intonation, however, was familiar—

its subject matter the end times. Ina imagined her father sliding a hand across the seat, through darkness and dust, to clasp Caroline's own in an attempt to still her hysterics. Ina thought again of the Whitman family, what it must have been like when their windshield succumbed and death came pouring in. Like an ill-lit scene in a moving picture show, Ina watched in her mind's eye as a perfect vortex of debris-filled wind stripped away their lives and sent them to that timeless place Jacob now called home.

Ina wasn't certain how long she had been caught up in this reverie before she heard a heavy banging on the door opposite to her own, along with what sounded like a cry for help. Due to the force of the wind, she knew it would be impossible to open the door, but she couldn't resist sliding across the seat as if making ready to do so. She placed her ear to the rattling window but heard nothing beyond the roaring, grit-filled ocean of wind doing its best to strip the coupe's skin and get at its more precious meat.

Ina tucked deeper into herself and tried to think of brighter, more hopeful days, of memories filled only with joy. But her thoughts kept returning to Jacob, lost as he had been in a storm such as this, perishing alone. Part of her wished she could join him, use some inner strength to open the door and allow the storm to usher her into the void. But she had her family to consider—they needed her as much as she needed them. There was nothing she could do now but wait and listen and hope that the storm would give up before she did.

"It's loosening," her father muttered after a time, his voice clearer now.

Ina could make out her parents' silhouettes, and the coupe had ceased its rough-sea rocking—clear signs that the weather was shifting. What had not changed, what had become even more pronounced, was Imogene. She still seemed caught in the horrors of the storm, and Caroline could do little to placate the newborn.

Henry engaged the windshield wiper, creating a bright swath across the dust-coated glass. Light flooded into the coupe, and after Ina's eyes adjusted, she had a clear glimpse of the road ahead. It looked like nothing she remembered. Drifts of fine soil were cast everywhere, leaving only a snaking bit of roadway that disappeared and reappeared like a half-buried serpent. Ina turned around, finding a small opening in the darkened back window. Through this camera obscura, she was able to glimpse the tail-end of the storm as it swept south. It was one of the most frightening and beautiful sights she had ever seen, and it was a miracle that her family had survived, that the windows had not blown in, that the dust had not filled their innards like taxidermy for the sheriff to find.

"Henry!" Caroline called. "Someone's outside!"

Ina turned, following the direction of her mother's trembling finger. Her father was already making his way out, pushing at the door with some effort due to the collected dust. He trudged as best he could across the sandy, uneven landscape. When he arrived at the figure half-buried in the soil, he dropped to his knees and pulled it out like some overgrown, deformed vegetable. He clasped the child to his chest and ran back to the vehicle. Ina soon determined it was a young boy.

Caroline spoke, as though awakening from a dream, her words giving name to the portrait now blossoming in Ina's mind.

"Jacob," she cried. "Oh, dear god, Jacob . . . "

WHAT AWAITED THEM at home surprised no one, least of all Ina. They had endured numerous storms, and the far-reaching dust never failed to breach the walls and roof of the farmhouse, painting nearly every surface with a fine powder. No matter how diligent they were—caulking or taping susceptible areas such as windows and doors—the dust always managed to find a way in. The attic was the worst. Often, after a duster had passed, Ina would stand in the living room and watch mesmerized as sheets of grit streamed down the walls with the consistency of a waterfall. It was oddly soothing, if you could get past the mess it made, like watching sand fall through an hourglass.

In the weeks and months between storms, the clean-up never seemed to end. Ina did her best to assist in each recovery, but she sensed in her mother a growing depression. She had heard of two other women in the county who had taken their lives because of the stark impossibility of keeping a clean home. Jacob's disappearance, as well as the dust pneumonia that afflicted Imogene, had cut deep into the stitchwork of Caroline's sanity. There seemed little that Ina could do to brighten her mother's despair. The picnic, which had been her idea, had helped, if only temporarily. But with Jacob's improbable return, her mother's eyes had returned to their normal lucidity, glowing with hope.

While it was certain that Jacob was alive—his breathing was as steady as any of their own, save for Imogene—he had yet to respond to their pleas. According to Henry, the boy was in a coma, and that seemed as good an explanation as any. He had been lost to a duster over a month ago, his body never recovered. But how could he have survived so long on the open plains? Had the sands sustained him, preserved his body like a cocoon? It was a ridiculous and fanciful notion, but one to which Jacob himself would have subscribed. He'd always been the imaginative one, the storyteller of the family, and Ina had little doubt that he would have achieved great fame through his stories. She still had a few of them that he'd written, tucked safely in the box beneath her bed.

But what to make of this new Jacob's eyes? They never closed and were as black as a duster's heart. Ina had heard survivor tales of others caught in a storm, their eyes layered with so much dust that they were eventually struck blind. But with her brother, it was different. She had stared at those weird eyes most of the way home, experiencing a prickling of fear as she did so. When they arrived at the farm, her mother's first task was to clean Jacob's face with a wet cloth, then dowse those obsidian eyes in the hope of renewing the blue they once contained. But the more she tried, the brighter those black orbs shone, as polished as marbles. In time, Caroline had dropped her head in despair and wept, departing the room.

Now, as Ina studied Jacob, she felt a chill. How could this possibly be her brother? If it weren't for the eyes, Ina might have been convinced of a miraculous resurrection. She thought of summoning her father, mostly because she did not want to sit here alone. But he was currently removing drifts of dust that had collected in the kitchen and living room, and someone needed to remain at Jacob's side in case he woke up. Ina tried to think of something witty to say, certain that she'd be able to penetrate the depths of his trance, but she felt numb, her thoughts a broiling duster of confusion. Eventually, she leaned in close and whispered, "You in there, Jake?"

Her brother's steady breathing continued, and there was nothing in his deathlike demeanor to suggest he had heard her voice. Most unnerving of all was that he seemed to be staring intently at the ceiling. While it was obvious that he was not awake, Ina had a feeling that Jacob was aware of his surroundings. She had always felt a strong connection to him, as if she could read his thoughts. They were the exact age, born on the same April day. But now there was a blank slate, nothing inside him that she could decipher other than this near-supernatural alertness. She placed a hand over his, surprised by the warmth. His pulse, when she found it, startled her.

"How'd you do it, Jake?" she asked. "How'd you make it through?"

A moment later, Caroline returned and asked that she and Jacob be left alone. Imogene was nuzzled against her bosom, coughing in her sleep. Ina was grateful for the reprieve, and she withdrew to help her father with the dust. Part of her wished, however, to remain, for she sensed that Jacob would soon awaken.

IT HAD TAKEN all afternoon and much of the evening to restore the house to a livable condition, though it was by no means free of dust. Caroline had remained in Jacob's room all the while, leaving Ina to fend for herself when it came to preparing dinner. She fashioned a plate of casserole and biscuits for her father and herself, then brought a helping to the other room. Her mother seemed intent on spending the night with Jacob, so Ina offered to take responsibility of Imogene.

"But you look so tired, dear," Caroline said, her tone uncharacteristically buoyant. "You should try and get some sleep. Tomorrow's a new day."

While Ina wanted nothing more than to stay and ask after Jacob— there were so many things she needed to know—she knew better than to question the wisdom behind the words. She stepped to her mother's side, kissed her lightly on the cheek, and whispered that she loved her dearly. Maybe she would be able to speak with Jacob tomorrow. Surely his dark slumber will have lifted by then.

Sleep was hard to find most nights, but that evening Ina found it impossible to drift away. It didn't feel right knowing that Jacob, or the thing that so closely resembled him, was in the next room. She couldn't resist placing an ear to the thin adjoining wall, listening for further signs of life, waiting for Jacob's call. More than once during the long night, she had snuck to the threshold of his room, merely to see if he was still there. If she was truthful, the real reason she could not fall asleep was that she was terrified of losing him again.

Now, Ina stared at the ceiling and listened to the wind as it intensified against her windowpane. A storm was close, but she felt paralyzed, as though caught in a dream, unable to rise and warn her parents of the approaching duster. At some point—minutes or hours later, she could not tell—she became aware of a presence looming quietly at her side. Someone was studying her, and she knew intuitively it was Jacob. She reached into the darkness and, in turn, a dust-coated hand clasped her own. And in the next impossible moment . . .

. . . *she is flying, soaring through the dark as dust-grit scours her flesh. There is no pain, only a tickling sensation as though being misted by cool water on a sun-scorched day. There is darkness here, though she can see through it all, see farms, cattle, cars, and all the various other detritus that litters the land, including country folk caught out in the storm. Jacob is inside her, or she is inside him, it's hard to say. They soar with ease through the raging maelstrom, and in the distance, she sees a town. She tries to speak, to ask Jacob what is happening, but she exists only within vision, an impossible perception that allows her to see everything, even the kin-like things that careen as they do through the currents of the storm, things drawn toward a sustenance she can only feel in the pit of her (or Jacob's) stomach. There's playfulness in their flight, but also the seriousness of the hunter. Their arms and stout jaws seem to elongate in the stress of the storm, and at one point a group of them break free and shoot like arrows toward the earth, in the direction of town and whatever sustenance awaits them there. One of the things appears at her side before its descent, its obsidian eyes curious, pausing long enough for her*

to catch a glimpse of its sleek, humanoid face. It shares a knowing smile
before it disappears, replaced by another layer of darkness that blinds
her. In the void, she becomes aware of a familiar, pleading voice . . .

"Ina . . . Ina, dear . . . wake up. "

She opened her eyes and saw her father crouching before her,
his concerned expression lit by the weak glow of an oil lamp. He
had her by the shoulders, giving her a shake as she slowly resurfaced
from whatever possession had afflicted her. How long had she been
away? More to the point: *had* she been away? She noticed her
mother standing next to Henry, smiling but tearful. The lamp's
flickering flame cast her features in a ghostly light, as though at
any moment she might disappear.

"*Jacob* . . . " she moaned, her voice desperate. She withdrew into
further darkness and continued to weep. The wind seemed louder
now. Ina turned her attention to her father, waiting for him to explain.

"Jacob's gone, honey." He rose to his feet, encouraging her from
bed. They stepped into the kitchen, to the dinner table where the
oil lamp was set. The wind howled under the door and against the
windows and roof. Ina knew she had to tell her father what she
had experienced, to explain that Jacob lived now in the storm, in the
dust. She knew that her parents were not prepared for such fantasy,
that they would be angered by her crude rationalization of Jacob's
disappearance. In all honesty, how could her flight through the
dust be construed as anything other than a dream? Even now, back

on the ground and safe in her parents' arms, Ina found it impossible to believe that her experience held any merit in reality.

Caroline, who still kept to the shadows, could not stop weeping. "I *won't* do this again, *won't* lose him again," she said, nearly hyperventilating. Ina watched her, wondering if she should go to her, comfort her. She wondered if it would help, or if her mother was lost for good. Suddenly, Caroline's focus shifted to the door, and she strode to it, grasping the handle, ready to invite the maelstrom in. Henry was quick to act, but not fast enough. The door exploded inward and plumes of dust burst inside, flooding the space like grain into a bin. Caroline didn't get farther than the threshold before she was thrown violently back, falling to the floor near the table. Henry struggled desperately to close the door, succeeding only after Ina pitched in to help. With her back against the heaving slab, she was left staring at the pitiful specter that was her mother, and it made her sick to her stomach.

"*Jacob* . . . " Caroline repeatedly moaned, crawling toward the door, wanting to be free, wanting to step beyond where death would gladly have her.

WITHIN AN HOUR the storm was gone, the sun returned to its mantle of blue. Caroline was on the porch with Imogene, scanning the newly shaped landscape in search of Jacob. Ina remained inside, preparing breakfast after she and her father had cleared as much dust from the kitchen as possible. Her mother rarely helped with cleanup anymore, convinced it was no longer necessary, no longer a worthwhile endeavor. Henry, on the other hand, remained resigned to a fault, rarely if ever shedding a complaint. To him, the cleanup was another labor, as essential as ministering to one's (now-defunct) fields. Most of their crops had been destroyed by locusts or jackrabbits, two scavengers who alone seemed to thrive on the apocalyptic plains. Too bad there wasn't a market for dust, Henry had often joked, because then they'd live like kings. Ina knew that deep down her father hadn't adapted to any of it, even if his stoic veneer told otherwise.

After breakfast, Henry rose from the table and announced that he was going out in search of Jacob. Ina turned from the sink, wash-rag in hand. "I'm coming, too."

Henry shook his head. "You're needed here," he said and nodded resolutely toward Imogene and Caroline, entrusting to Ina the all-important task of watching over them. Then he was off, pushing through the screen door and leaving Ina feeling useless and numb.

But not for long. Ina stepped to her mother's side and clasped her shoulder. "I'm going," she whispered, glowing with a defiance she doubted Caroline even recognized. No motherly rebuttal ever came, and in the growing silence, Ina backstepped from the table, hurt that she was not being listened to, that her mother was not even aware of her disobedience.

Outside, she stood at the edge of the porch, sighting her father in the far distance. She bolted after him, feeling as though she were floating atop the land, over soil that had drifted so high that in certain spots it bridged the top of a barbed-wire fence. She stilled an impulse to glance to her right, at the thing she had glimpsed in the corner of her eye. The recently deceased cattle deserved better, and Ina didn't understand why her father allowed them to rot so long. She increased her pace as best she could along the dust-slippery landscape. Now and again, jackrabbits would burst from their hiding spots. Just last month, Ina had witnessed the cruelty of the jackrabbit drives in town, watched as hundreds of the penned creatures were clubbed not only by men but by boys her age and younger. She hadn't been able to watch for long and was angry at her father for days afterward for taking her to see such wholesale slaughter. A plague of these verminous creatures had spread far and wide since the storms had begun, so Ina could understand the need to be rid of them, but that didn't mean she had to take part or even like it. The thing that disturbed her most was the savageness of the participants. It made her regard her neighbors in a new, more disturbing light.

Her father had stopped and turned in his tracks so that he faced toward home, arms akimbo, as if this gesture would be warning enough to send Ina scurrying back. But it didn't deter her in the least, and when she arrived at her father's side neither of them spoke. She surveyed the disorienting landscape for any sign of Jacob, knowing all the while that he would not be found, and when she looked into her father's eyes, she knew his assessment was not far off from her own. She shielded her eyes with her hand and continued to examine the land, vague memories resurfacing of a time when it had looked so different, when the surface of the world she had been born into had not contained a sea of sand but a genuine and undulating land filled with a plethora of prairie grass. The past seemed more like a dream these days than memory, for Ina hadn't been much older than Imogene when the transformations had first begun. Even under such worsening conditions, Henry had no intention of ever giving up on the farm. Her ever-hopeful father, whose unwavering mantra was that *next year* things would improve, *next year* a decent life-sustaining crop would produce, *next year* the land and their hearts would heal. Always *next year*.

Ina's own abiding and desperate hope was that her father would come to his senses and move the family to town. It would be better there, with friends and among folk fighting this new world together. The isolation of their farm wouldn't have been so bad had the land been healthy, but Henry's refusal to leave, his stubborn and impractical outlook, would not be swayed, no matter how rationally Ina might plead. So for now, they would plod ahead *together*, make do *together*, until things improved. They need only remain steadfast and hold out for longer, *one more year*. The rains would come, *next year*, and when they did this land would produce a bounty never before seen. Ina half-believed her father when he spoke so grandly. She trusted that he knew things she did not, though she had to admit that this trust had nearly eroded, like a house made of dust.

"Time to head back," her father said, his voice low. Ina heard other words beneath the surface: *Jacob's not here. The land has him now. For good.*

So she trailed her father's long strides toward home, and when they arrived they found Caroline sitting on the porch steps, gazing despondently at a hastily-erected mound of dirt a few feet away. A portion of Imogene's face and doll-like hands were visible, but the rest of her was covered by dust. Henry bolted forward, and as he ripped the child from the makeshift grave, Ina could tell by its drooping limbs and reflecting skin that it was as lifeless as the dust that made up this cruel, cruel world.

HENRY WAS HAVING difficulty starting the coupe, so Ina stepped out to help him wipe dust from the exposed engine. Caroline sat inanimately in the front seat, Imogene swaddled tightly in a bright blue blanket at her side. The blanket was as beautiful as the sky and seemed already a part of it. Ina felt numb and clumsy and useless as she assisted her father, daring not to speak over his cursing whispers. She had never heard him use such words, ever. And hearing them now made her feel that the end of everything was near to hand. She felt alone, with no one to lean on, no one to lead her from a fast-approaching doom.

In time, as though triggered by Henry's harsh language alone, the coupe fired up, providing a boon to Ina's despair. As they made their slow trek to town, her father seemed more himself now, at least outwardly, but the silence in the car spoke volumes. He was holding on by a thread, and Ina prayed that the coupe would hold its course, for she sensed that were it to break down, her father would follow suit. Then she'd be stuck in the middle of this waste-land with no one but a ghost mother to keep her company. She needed her father, needed his strength, but there seemed little she could do to resurrect him. At times during the journey, she thought she heard Imogene crying or coughing inside her blue cocoon, and for long periods she nearly convinced herself that her kid sister had been cured of dust pneumonia and was merely sleeping. Caroline had not shifted an inch the entire while, had not checked to see how Ina or her father were doing. She merely stared blankly ahead, blind to all but her thoughts—if she even had any. Ina imagined the coupe as a casket, her mother embedded within.

As hard as she tried, Ina could no longer hold back tears. She turned and did her best to disappear into the corner of the dusty back seat, covering her mouth as her body juddered uncontrollably. She was embarrassed by the crying fit, for she had always thought herself strong, beyond the weaknesses of her mother. After a time, she thought she heard her father speak, asking if she was okay. She couldn't tell because her ears felt plugged with cotton. When she glanced his way, the only thing she noticed was his limp arms making minor adjustments to the wheel. Ina returned to her corner and slumped against the window, staring out of it like the rest of them.

She wasn't sure how much time passed.

AS THE COUPE downshifted and lumbered into town, Ina studied the residents and business folk going about their business. Hope returned to her, and she wished with all her heart that her family would never have to leave this place, wished that their farm was already buried in so much dust that it would never be found. She was happy to leave the past behind and to bury old memories. A new life awaited them here, and she sensed that she would never again face loneliness among such people. They had waged their war on dust and won. Ina smiled, hoping to catch the attention of a few of these hope-filled souls. She'd been to town before, but the place felt different this time around. Like a sanctuary.

Halfway down the street, Henry parked the coupe in front of Doc Parson's. Ina had only visited the doctor's office on one other occasion, after breaking her wrist a few years back while attempting to plow for the first time. She liked Doc, whose sage demeanor never failed to put a positive spin on the tragedies of life. If anyone could make things better in this world, it was him. His name printed across the front window in bold gold lettering was like a nostrum, making her feel exquisitely lightheaded.

"Wait here," Henry said, withdrawing from the vehicle and walking stiff-legged toward the two-story brick building.

Ina leaned over the front seat. "It's gonna be okay, Ma," she said. "Doc'll fix things up, you wait and see."

When her father returned, Doc Parsons was at his side. They helped Caroline from the car, and soon enough the trio was headed back to the office. Ina reluctantly followed, confused as to if she was expected to carry Imogene. She left the bundle behind and hastened toward the building, hardly able to still her emotions.

CAROLINE HAD BEEN taken to the hotel across the way, where she was presently resting in the relative quiet and comfort of a dust-free room. Doc Parsons had given her a sedative, stating that he wished to keep a close eye on her for the next few days. Some funeral men had already taken Imogene away, leaving Ina petrified to know what would become of her kid sister. She hoped her mother could summon the strength to return to this world, to shake the darkness that had enveloped her so long. First Jacob, then Imogene, and now her mother. All lost, torn from her life. How long before Henry joined and she was left truly alone? Doc Parsons had given him some pills, though Ina wasn't sure what they were for. Her father hadn't moved from the chair next to the bed, clasping Caroline's pale hand all the while.

To counter the encroaching darkness, Ina imagined scenarios of her mother's awakening, her previous depressions shed like dusty skin, and all of them moving forward together, rediscovering the joy that had eluded them so long. Ina remained cautiously optimistic about their future. As much as she desired Jacob's return, she also knew that whatever life now ran through his veins was not natural. He had been changed by means she could not fathom, his transformation more fantastic than any of the stories he had ever told or written down. His new existence terrified her, but at the same time, she longed to relive that flight through the dust, no matter how otherworldly it might seem. There was freedom associated with it, and a beautiful one at that, and her exposure, while frightening at first, made her realize that there was also a purity there, a purity hidden inside all that dust.

Ina leaned against the room's single window, through which she was afforded a clear view of Main Street. She grew mesmerized by the activity below, vehicles and citizenry moving to and fro. On the farm the only things imbued with such spirited resolve were jackrabbits. Ina turned briefly to her father, wanting to ask him if they were planning to stay for good, but now wasn't the right time. His focus remained on Caroline, and for now, that was good enough. Ina made a mental list of the things she wished to discuss with him, the benefits of city living, and the fact that she planned to take up any sort of work that became available, no matter how menial. She had no desire to go back to the pointless upkeep of their farm. Nothing but death awaited them there. A purposeful life could be had in this town, and she longed to be out there in the midst of it all. She turned to her father, who was already staring in her direction. His blank countenance spoke volumes, but his nod was acknowledgment enough for Ina to act.

She approached the bed, lightly grasping her mother's hand. "I'll be back soon, Mama," she said, remaining there until thoughts of life and death—and something that might exist in-between— threatened to overwhelm her. She broke free and hastened from the room, clambering down the stairs and out the front door to the wooden sidewalk that stretched unevenly along Main Street. She wandered for blocks, trying but failing to unburden herself of dark memories. Eventually, she stopped on the porch of a general store, stunned by the realization that she had not encountered a single soul since leaving the hotel. She studied her surroundings with a clearer eye, taken aback by what she did not see. Where was everyone? Cars were parked on either side of the street, with no concern as to their placement. The sky was darkening as well, as though evening were setting in. But that was impossible because she'd left the hotel at a little past noon. She was sure of it.

Ina heard a voice summoning her from across the street, but due to the growing darkness and wind, she had difficulty locating the individual in question. She stepped into the street and was halfway across when she noticed a beckoning silhouette. A few more steps and the woman became more fully defined. She was leaning out the double doors of the movie theater, demanding Ina to her side.

"Child, quick. It's nearly here."

The wind blew more forcefully now, but it was only when the grit of the approaching duster flooded into town that Ina knew she was in trouble. The town was hardly immune; why had she thought it ever was? It was the same storm-ravaged place it had always been and always would be, and she needed to find cover. She turned to her right and gazed at the mile-high wall of dust that was already obliterating the horizon, a mountain range come to life. It seemed more ominous than any of the previous dusters she'd seen. She felt paralyzed, stuck like a statue in the middle of the street.

The woman in the theater was calling more forcefully now, but Ina could no longer make out her words. The storm was the only voice now, uttering the command that mattered most. Ina turned, intending to run to the theater, but was startled to discover that the darkness had swallowed it whole. She shifted herself to face the storm, overwhelmed by an emotion she was not expecting: beauty. The storm was beguiling, inviting. It was, after all, Jacob's new home, and he was up there now, soaring carefree through all that dust. Without another thought, Ina began walking into the storm, toward Jacob, struggling to keep herself steady as the stinging winds tore at her skin. But she did not fear. It felt as though her brother and the wind and the darkness were all a combination of one thing, and she grew eager to learn this new progenitor's ways.

In the full dark, something clasped Ina's hand, and while her first impulse was to pull free, she knew it could be none other than Jacob. She allowed herself to be led forward, and it felt more than anything as if they were running again, she and her beautiful twin brother, sprinting carefree along the prairie of their childhood and into a brighter future. She noticed that her vision was changing—it had to be, for she was able to decipher the outlines of things previously hidden from view, and glimpse the world through newer, more sensitive orbs.

She could even see Jacob, so close to her side. His black eyes shone, his old skin stripped and the new one rich and glowing with life. The sensation of running soon transitioned to the exhilarating buoyancy of flight, and while Jacob was no longer holding her hand, Ina sensed his closeness and knew that from this moment forward she always would.

ABOUT THE AUTHOR

———◆———

C.M. MULLER lives in St. Paul, Minnesota with his wife and two sons—and, of course, all those quaint and curious volumes of forgotten lore. He is related to the Norwegian writer Jonas Lie and draws much inspiration from that scrivener of old. His tales have appeared in *Shadows & Tall Trees, Dim Shores, Vastarien,* and a host of other venues. In addition to writing, he also edits and publishes the journal *Nightscript*. His debut story collection, *Hidden Folk*, was released in 2018. *Secondary Roads* is his sophomore collection.

———◆———

For more information, please visit:

www.chthonicmatter.wordpress.com

PUBLICATION HISTORY

A Winter Reunion first appeared in:
Weirdbook #41 (2019)

Vanpool first appeared in:
Vastarien: A Literary Journal (2019)

Camera Obscura first appeared in:
Shadows & Tall Trees #8 (2020)

Descrambler first appeared in:
The New Flesh: A Tribute to David Cronenberg (2019)

The In-between appears here for the first time.

Duplex first appeared in:
Dark Lane Anthology #8 (2019)

In Demontreville appears here for the first time.

Marginalia appears here for the first time.

The Opposite Track first appeared in:
In Stefan's House: A Tribute to Stefan Grabinski (2019)

Cold Black Wind appears here for the first time.

An Illusion of Substance first appeared in:
Gorgon: Stories of Emergence (2019)

In the Dust first appeared in:
Dim Shores Presents:Volume 2 (2021)

Made in the USA
Monee, IL
03 October 2022

fa500a83-7573-4f06-a517-6e9bf5c6f2eeR01